"We can't deny t

"Or maybe I'm mi

"You're not misreading anything," Jason said.

Holly looked up at him, putting her mouth mere inches from his. Was she *trying* to drive him crazy? Or did it just come naturally?

"I think we'll agree that anything beyond friendship would be a bad idea," she said, so close he could feel the heat of her breath on his lips.

It took everything in him not to kiss her. To keep his libido in check. The only thing giving him the will to resist was the drowsy child lying limp in his arms. He was a much-needed buffer. "Are you always this brutally honest?"

"If we have any hope of making this work, if the boys and I are going to live under your roof, we have to be honest with each other. Even if the truth hurts a little."

Holly was still watching him, waiting for a response. If she wanted honesty, that was what he would give her. "The truth is, I really want to kiss you."

* * *

Demanding His Brother's Heirs
is part of Harlequin Desire's #1 bestselling series,
Billionaires and Babies: Powerful men...
wrapped around their babies' little fingers

Dear Reader,

This book was a loooong time in the making. I wrote it originally about eight years ago, but it wasn't what they were looking for at the time. I put the story aside, but the characters never completely left my mind. I could hear them in the background. Faintly at first, then louder. They would not be ignored. So I got to work reimagining their story.

I've known Holly and Jason for a long time, yet they still managed to surprise me. Their love story was truly an adventure for me, and I'm happy that you can share it.

Michelle

DEMANDING HIS BROTHER'S HEIRS

MICHELLE CELMER

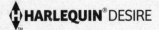

Recycling programs
for this product may
not exist in your area.

ISBN-13: 978-0-373-73402-3

Demanding His Brother's Heirs

Copyright © 2015 by Michelle Celmer

Printed in U.S.A.

Michelle Celmer is a bestselling author of more than thirty books. When she's not writing, she likes to spend time with her husband, kids, grandchildren and a menagerie of animals.

Michelle loves to hear from readers. Like her on Facebook or write her at PO Box 300, Clawson, MI 48017.

Books by Michelle Celmer

Harlequin Desire

The Nanny Bombshell
Princess in the Making
More Than a Convenient Bride
Demanding His Brother's Heirs

Black Gold Billionaires

The Tycoon's Paternity Agenda
One Month with the Magnate
A Clandestine Corporate Affair
Much More Than a Mistress

The Caroselli Inheritance

Caroselli's Christmas Baby
Caroselli's Baby Chase
Caroselli's Accidental Heir

Visit the Author Profile page at Harlequin.com for more titles.

To new beginnings

One

Holly Shay didn't believe in signs.

But as she tossed Devon's and Marshall's dirty clothes on top of the hamper, her wedding band, loose after she'd dropped the last of her baby weight, slipped off her finger and went flying across the room. Two carats of flawless princess-cut diamonds hit the wall at high velocity, leaving a dimple in the paint, and landed with a clunk on the nursery floor.

Maybe someone was trying to tell her something. That it was time to take it off. At this point she didn't have much choice.

The idea of hocking the ring broke her heart, but she had only a few weeks to find a new apartment. She had no job and not a penny to her name. Only after Jeremy's death last month had she learned of the considerable debt he'd sunk them into over the course of their ten-month marriage. She would be paying off his debts for many years to come.

But that's what addicts did, or so she had been told. If she had only known she could have helped him. It still astounded her that she had been so blind. She'd known deep down that something wasn't quite right with him. She'd assumed it was the stress of having twin infants. A new marriage—especially the shotgun variety—was a challenge in itself, but toss a high-risk pregnancy, then fragile preemies into the mix and things could get dicey. The boys had been born a month early and had had to spend nearly two weeks in the NICU. When they finally had come home it had been with machines to monitor their breathing and heart rate. It had taken a toll on them both.

But it wasn't until after Jeremy overdosed that she'd put the pieces of the puzzle together. Only then did she recognize the signs. She had been stupidly and irresponsibly blinded by love, by the fantasy of the perfect family she had always dreamed of having. When would she learn that for some people the happily-ever-after would never come? It just wasn't in the game plan.

It could have been so much worse. Holly had lost both her parents when she was a child, but she had been one of the lucky ones. Orphaned ten-year-olds typically were difficult to place in the foster care system, but she had been taken in by a really nice couple with two other foster kids. There never had been much money, but the essentials always had been covered. She'd had a hot meal every night, decent clothes on her back and someone to help with her homework. And though she and her foster siblings all lived at opposite ends of the country now, and her foster parents had retired to Florida, they still emailed and texted on a semi-regular basis. But it wasn't the same as having a real family.

The last pinkish whispers of dusk filtered through the blinds as Holly gazed down into the matching cribs at her sleeping sons. An overwhelming feeling of love filled the chambers of her heart. She'd never known it was possible to feel such an intense connection to another person. She would hands down give her life for them.

They would be three months old tomorrow, meaning Jeremy had been gone almost a month now. It broke her heart that they would never know their father. Her marriage to Jeremy hadn't been perfect, or easy, but the good relationships never were. She just hadn't realized how *im*perfect it actually had been.

Was it better that he had died now rather than in a year or two? Had not knowing him spared the twins undue heartache? Or would they go through life with a hole in their hearts that never would be filled?

Could you miss someone you'd never known?

Holly remembered all too well what it had been like after her parents died. She had learned to cope, but it was the sort of thing a person never really got over. It was always in the back of her mind. The unfairness of it. The deep feeling of emptiness. Knowing that she was truly alone. But now that she had the boys, she would never be alone again.

She walked across the room to where the ring had landed and bent over to pick it up. It had always felt clunky and heavy on her hand. Too big and flashy. That was Jeremy's taste, not hers. She would have been content with one carat or less. He'd refused to tell her what it cost, but it must have been thousands. Tens of thousands, even. Hopefully it was worth at least half that much used.

Instead of sliding the ring back on her finger, she slipped it into the front pocket of her jeans. The landlord had taken pity on her and given her an entire month rent-free to get her affairs in order and find an affordable place. She couldn't put it off any longer. Tomorrow morning she would load the boys in the stroller and take a trip to the jewelers to see what she could get for the ring. She'd run the scenario through her head a million times, and the outcome was always the same. She needed money, and the ring was the only thing she had left of any worth. She didn't even own a car. Which made hauling twins around a challenge.

The only question now was, even if she had the money to get a new apartment, would anyone give her a lease? The credit cards Jeremy had opened in her name were all maxed out and in default, and until she could arrange for some sort of child care, getting a job would be next to impossible. She had no family to help her, no friends willing to take on the task of twins full time, and conventional day care for two infants would be astronomically expensive.

In her chest she felt a tightness, a knot of despair that made it hard to breathe. She'd been through difficult times in the past, but never had she felt this hopeless, this sense of impending doom.

She peered into the cribs one last time, smiling when her gaze settled on the boys' sweet angelic faces. Then she turned on the baby monitor and backed out of the nursery, quietly shutting the door behind her.

She and Jeremy had seriously discussed moving but they'd never gotten the chance. Her morning sickness had been so bad the first four months Holly had spent half her time in bed, and the other half hanging over the commode. In her fifth month, just as she had begun to feel like a human being again, she had gone into premature labor. They'd stopped it just in time, but from that day on she'd been on strict bed rest. It hadn't been easy, but they'd managed. At least, she'd thought they had.

Jeremy had promised her that after the boys were born they would start looking for a house. He'd thought they would buy a fixer-upper in a small cozy town upstate. A place they could make their own. Now she knew that with all of Jeremy's debt, no bank ever would have given them a mortgage. Jeremy must have known it, too.

She felt torn between missing him and wanting to sock him in the nose for not being honest with her. Whatever their problems, they could have worked them out. Why hadn't he just talked to her? It was no secret he'd had trust issues, but they had run deeper than she'd realized. A foster kid himself, Jeremy hadn't been as lucky. He hadn't talked about his past much, but she knew he'd been in the system most of his life, bounced around between group homes and foster homes until he'd ventured out on his own at sixteen. Clearly his past had scarred him more than she'd ever imagined. As his wife she should have known. She should have seen what was happening, right? She could have saved him.

The question was had he wanted to be saved?

She stepped into her bedroom and switched on the light. Their neatly made king-size bed mocked her from across the room. She hadn't slept in it since she'd found Jeremy there. Other than straightening the covers, she hadn't touched it at all. She'd been avoiding the bedroom in general, only going in to grab her clothes, and only because there was no place else in the apartment to store them. She'd been sleeping on an air mattress that she'd first put in the nursery, and recently moved into the living room next to the sofa.

She looked around the room and sighed. She used to love this apartment. Now she could barely wait to leave. Since his death being here felt...wrong. It never would be a home again without Jeremy. His whole life, everything he'd owned in the world, was in that apartment. She was torn between wanting to keep it all and the need for a fresh start.

She grabbed her pajamas and pulled the door closed behind her as she stepped into the hall. It was barely eight o'clock, but these days she slept when the boys slept. That wouldn't be possible when she got a job.

She collapsed onto the sofa, letting her head fall back and her eyes slip closed. She must have gone out instantly, and when she roused to the sound of a knock at the door, it was nearly nine-thirty.

She assumed the visitor was her neighbor Sara from across the hall, who often stopped by after work to chat, so Holly didn't bother checking the peephole. She wasn't exactly in the mood for company, but it would be rude not to say hello.

She pulled open the door, but it wasn't Sara, after all. A man stood there, and though he was facing away, looking down the hall toward the stairs, something about him seemed eerily familiar. Something about the tall, solid build and broad shoulders. The thick, coarse black hair that swirled into a cowlick at the left side of his crown, and the stubborn little tuft that wanted to stand up straight. He would always have to use extra gel—

Her breath caught in her lungs and her heart took a downward dive to the pit of her belly. Oh, God. Whoever this man was, from the back he looked exactly like Jeremy. Except for the clothes. He wore a suit, and Holly had worked in retail long enough to recognize a custom fit when she saw one. The closest Jeremy had ever come to wearing a suit, custom or otherwise, had been dress slacks and a blazer, and then only because she'd forbade him from wearing jeans to the wedding of a good friend. And she'd had to go out and buy the stuff for him.

She'd barely completed the thought when the man turned, and as she saw his face, her world shifted violently. Staring back at her were eyes as familiar as her own, and though she could see his lips moving, his voice sounded muffled and distant, as if someone had stuffed cotton in her ears. Her vision blurred around the edges, then folded in on itself.

It couldn't be, she told herself. Either she was dreaming or having a complete psychotic break. Because this man didn't just look like her dead husband.

He *was* Jeremy.

Before Jason Cavanaugh could inquire as to the identity of the attractive blonde who'd opened the door to the apartment his lawyer claimed had been his brother's, the color leached from her face. Then her eyes went wide and rolled back into her head. He watched helplessly as she crumpled to the floor, her head barely missing the door frame as she went down.

He sighed and mumbled a curse. His prowess with women was legendary, but even he'd never had one fall to his feet in a dead faint.

As an identical twin, this wouldn't be the first time someone had mistaken him for his brother. Though he had never gotten this reaction before. Angry words, yes, and once he'd even had a drink thrown in his face.

He could only imagine what Jeremy had done to this poor girl. Had he charged up all her credit cards and then bailed on her? Slept with her best friend? Or her mother? Or her best friend's mother?

When it came to Jeremy the possibilities were endless. But all Jason wanted was to fetch his brother's belongings, if they hadn't been disposed of already, and head back upstate. He didn't know if there was anything worth keeping, and he wasn't normally the sentimental type, but he had so little left of his brother. Five years ago, after Jeremy had been through another wasted stint in rehab, their father had had enough. He'd disowned Jeremy, disinherited him and purged their home of anything that reminded him of his troubled son. For all the good it had done. And though he knew it was irrational, deep down Jason still blamed himself for Jeremy's downward spiral. Against his father's wishes, Jason had even set up a monthly allowance for his brother, who had no means to support himself. Maybe that had been a mistake, too.

Jason knelt beside the woman, whom he was guessing couldn't be more than twenty-two or three, and touched her cheek. It was warm and it seemed the color was returning to her face. Long brown hair with reddish highlights fanned out around her head and her T-shirt rode up exposing an inch or so of her stomach, making him feel like a voyeur.

"Hey." He gave her shoulder a gentle nudge and she mumbled incoherently. "Wake up."

Her eyes fluttered open, big and blue and full of confusion as they focused on his face. "What happened?"

"You passed out," he said, offering his hand. "Can you sit up?"

"I think so." She grabbed on, her eyes glued to his

face, containing a look caught somewhere between shock and horror. He gave her a gentle boost and though she wobbled a little, squeezing his hand to keep her balance, she managed to stay upright.

"Got it?" he asked.

She nodded and let go, still transfixed. "You look just like him. Except…" She reached up to touch his left brow, grazing it with the tips of her fingers. Her touch was so light it was almost provocative. "No scar."

"No scar," he responded.

She blinked several times, then yanked her hand back, as if just realizing that she was touching a total stranger. "I'm sorry. I just…"

"It's okay." However or wherever Jeremy had gotten the scar, it must have occurred in the past five years. Since the day they were born, it had been next to impossible to tell them apart. They were truly identical in every way.

Well, almost every way.

"Jeremy never told you that he had an identical twin?"

She shook her head, appearing dazed and very confused. "He told me that he didn't have *any* family."

Jason was living proof that he had.

"He lied to me," she said, still shaking her head in disbelief. She looked up at Jason, and in her eyes he could see anger and hurt and a whole lot of confusion. "Why would he do that?"

Jason had asked himself that same question a million times. His brother was dead, and Jason was still cleaning up his messes. He would make amends on Jeremy's behalf. As he had done so many times in the past.

"Maybe I could come in and we could talk," he said, as it was a little awkward crouched down, half in, half out of the apartment. They clearly needed to get a dialogue going so he could assess the damage. However Jeremy had wronged this woman, Jason would fix it.

"Yes, of course," she said.

He rose to his feet and held out a hand to help her. "Need a boost?"

She nodded and, clinging firmly to his hand, slowly rose. She was taller than he'd expected. Maybe five-seven or -eight, putting her at his chin level. She was also excessively thin to the point of looking gaunt, with dark hollows under her eyes.

Jason felt a twinge of reservation. Was she strung out and in need of a fix? Had she supplied drugs to his brother, or had it been the other way around?

Whoa. Wait a minute.

He took a mental step back. He didn't know anything about this woman. It wasn't fair to assume she was into drugs just because his brother had been. That would be guilt by association, of which he himself had been a victim.

She wobbled slightly and he gripped her forearm with his other hand to steady her. "Take it slow."

Still dazed and looking pale, she said, "Maybe I should sit down."

"That's probably not a bad idea." She teetered on long slender legs encased in distressed, figure-hugging denim as he helped her to the sofa several feet away. That was when he saw the mostly empty baby bottles on the coffee table.

Jesus. His brother had sunk low enough to prey on a *single mother*? She wasn't wearing a wedding ring.

The idea made Jason sick to his stomach.

He sat on the edge of the coffee table across from

her, close enough to catch her if she passed out again. "Have you known Jeremy long?"

"A little over a year."

"And you two were…involved?"

She frowned. "He didn't tell you that he was married?"

Married? *Jeremy?* That was truly a shock. "No, he didn't. I haven't talked to my brother in more than five years. Since our father cut him off."

"Then you don't know about the boys."

"Boys?"

"Our sons. Devon and Marshall."

Two

If Jason hadn't already been sitting, the news would have knocked him off his feet. As it was, he felt as if someone had stolen the breath from his lungs.

He'd come here hoping to find a personal memento that would remind him of his brother. An article of clothing, maybe a photograph or two.

Never in his wildest dreams had he expected to find offspring. "My brother had *children*?"

"Twins."

"How old?"

"Nearly three months."

Oh, Jeremy, what have you done? "I'm sorry. I had no idea."

"So the boys have a real family? Aunts and uncles and cousins?"

She looked so hopeful he hated to burst her bubble. From the shadows under her eyes, and her painfully thin appearance, he was guessing life hadn't been kind to her lately. "We have distant relatives in the UK, but I'm the only one of our immediate family left."

"Oh. I don't have family, either, so I thought…" Her obvious disappointment tugged his heartstrings. But then she took a deep breath and forced a smile. Maybe she wasn't as fragile as she appeared. "But they do have you to tell them about their father. You probably knew Jeremy better than anyone."

Most of the time he felt as if he hadn't known Jeremy at all. Not since they'd been kids at least. "What exactly did he tell you about our family?"

"He told me that he had no family. He said he was orphaned as a toddler and grew up in the foster system."

Foster system? Nothing could have been further from the truth. But that was typical for Jeremy.

Jason tamped down the anger building inside him. "What else did he tell you?"

"That he was sick as a child, and because of his illness no one wanted him."

Jason's hackles stood at attention. "Did he say what sort of illness he had?"

"Cancer. He always feared it would come back."

Jason ground his teeth and tried to keep his cool.

"Jeremy did not have cancer. Nor did he grow up in foster care."

They had been raised by their biological parents in a penthouse apartment in Manhattan. There was little he and his brother wanted that they hadn't received. Maybe that had been part of the problem. Jeremy had never had to work for anything.

"He lied to me?" she asked, looking so pale and dumbfounded he worried she might pass out again. "Why?"

"Because that's what Jeremy does." He paused and corrected himself. "Or *did*."

A flash of pain crossed her face, and he felt like a jerk for being so insensitive. She obviously had cared deeply for his brother. But if their marriage was anything like his brother's past romantic relationships, this poor woman didn't know the real Jeremy. "They determined that it was an accidental overdose?"

Teeth wedged into her plump lower lip, she nodded. Her voice was unsteady when she said, "It was a lethal mix of prescription medication."

Jeremy would ingest just about anything that gave him a buzz, but prescription meds had always been his drugs of choice.

"You don't look surprised," she said.

"His addiction was the reason our father cut him off. The arrests, the months he spent in rehab… Nothing helped. He didn't know what else to do." Their father had exhausted every connection he had to keep Jeremy out of jail, when incarceration might have been the best thing for him.

"Why didn't I see it?" she asked, and in her eyes Jason saw a pain, a confusion, that he knew all too well.

"He was good at hiding it."

"At first I thought he was sleeping." Her eyes welled and she inhaled sharply, blinking back the tears. "They tried to revive him, but it was too late."

"There was nothing you could have done. I know it's difficult, but please don't blame yourself."

"That's easy for you to say."

"No, it's not." The way Jeremy behaved was in fact partly due to Jason, and he would never let himself forget that. Although, parallel with the pain of Jeremy's death flowed the relief that he would never hurt anyone again. He wouldn't be around to break his wife's heart. His children would be spared the pain of watching their father self-destruct. His wife was young and pretty, so it was unlikely she would stay single for long. Though the idea of another man raising his brother's children burned like a knife in his side. If anyone was going to take on the responsibility of raising Jeremy's kids, it would be Jason.

He opened his mouth to address her and realized he didn't even know her name. Nor had he told her his. "In all the excitement we weren't properly introduced," he said.

That earned him a cautious smile. "I guess we weren't. I'm Holly Shay."

"Jason Cavanaugh."

He offered his hand and she shook it, hitting him with another confused look. "Cavanaugh? But Jeremy said his last name—" She caught herself, shaking her head in disbelief. "But it wasn't Shay, was it? That was a lie, too."

"You're not the first woman with whom Jeremy—" He hesitated, searching for the least painful explanation "—misrepresented himself."

"So our relationship, our marriage, it was all one big lie?"

Now she was getting the idea. "Have there been financial repercussions?"

She hesitated, but the brief flash of fear and desperation in her eyes was all the answer he needed. Cheating strangers was one thing, but to con his own wife, the mother of his children? "How much did he take you for?"

She lowered her eyes, and when she didn't answer he asked, "Did he leave you in debt?"

With her lip wedged firmly between her teeth, she nodded.

"Considerable debt?"

Again, no answer.

"You can tell me the truth. It isn't going to upset me or hurt my feelings. I accepted a long time ago the sort of man my brother had become. Nothing you can say will shock me." Sadly, that was the honest truth.

She finally looked him in the eye, chin held high, and said, "I'm devastated financially. The only thing of value that I have left is my wedding ring. If it's even a real diamond."

At the mention of a ring Jason sat up straighter. Could it be possible? "Can I see it?"

"I have it right here actually." She reached into the front pocket of her jeans and pulled out the ring. Jason's heart skipped a beat. And here he'd thought that was gone forever, too. Traded for cash or drugs or God knew what else. He'd be damned if Jeremy had had a conscience after all.

"It's definitely real," he told her.

"How can you tell?"

"Because this ring belonged to my mother."

Holly was so screwed.

That ring had been her only hope to claw her way out of this financial abyss, but knowing that it had belonged to Jason's deceased mother she couldn't sell it now. She wouldn't be able to live with herself.

"Jeremy was the oldest by seven minutes, so when our mother died it went to him," Jason said. "It's been in our family for generations."

And that's where it should stay.

With a heavy heart, she held out the ring to Jason. "You should have this back."

"You're Jeremy's wife," he said. "The mother of his children. It belongs to you now."

If only that were true. She may have been his wife, but she obviously hadn't had a clue who he was. "Please, just take it."

Looking uncertain, Jason took the ring. "Are you sure?"

"Absolutely."

The thick platinum band and enormous stones looked so small in his big hand. "Honestly, I figured Jeremy had probably sold it years ago. I never thought I would see it again."

He slipped it into the inside pocket of his suit jacket. With it went all of her hopes and dreams of a decent start for her and her boys. What would she do now? File bankruptcy? Go on public assistance? Live in a shelter? Or on the street in a cardboard box?

Jason must have sensed her distress. His brow furrowed with concern, he asked, "Are you okay?"

"Fine," she said, pasting on a good face, the way she had for Jeremy, who'd never questioned the sincerity of her words. He'd believed anything she'd told him if it meant keeping the peace. Especially near the end.

Jason was clearly not at all like his brother.

"You don't look fine," he said, studying her, his eyes and his face, even his expression, so much like Jeremy's, but different somehow. "If it's money you're worried about, don't."

Someone had to. And talk of her dismal finances was making her uncomfortable.

"My money issues are really not your problem," she

said, letting him off the hook, thinking that would end the conversation.

"I'm making them my problem," he said firmly.

Whoa. His look said he wasn't playing around, but neither was she. "That's not necessary, but I appreciate the offer."

It was as if he hadn't even heard her. "I'll take care of your debt and give you whatever you need to get back on your feet."

Nope, not gonna happen. From the time she'd left her foster home until she'd married Jeremy, she'd survived completely on her own. It hadn't always been easy, but she'd managed. It was clear now that trusting Jeremy with their finances had been a terrible mistake. One she wouldn't be making again with anyone else. For all she knew Jason could be like his brother. He *seemed* genuine, but so had Jeremy. "I can't let you do that."

He watched her intently for several seconds, as if he were trying to decide if he could change her mind. Apparently he didn't think so. "If that's what you want."

"It is." She would get by somehow. She always had. Of course, back then, she hadn't had twin infants to consider.

"At least allow me to cover the funeral costs," he said. "I owe Jeremy that much. And his children."

If she let him it would shave off a fair chunk of her current financial responsibility. And maybe it would bring Jason closure. Everyone deserved that, right?

She shoved her pride aside long enough to say, "That would be okay."

He looked both sad and relieved. He was extremely attractive, but of course she would think that since he looked just like her husband, whose chiseled features and long lean physique had caught her eye the instant he'd walked into the party where they'd met. She'd never slept with a man on the first date, but she had gone home with him that night.

The sex itself hadn't been mind-blowing, but it had been nice. What she'd really liked, even more than the physical part, was just being near him. She'd liked the way his lips moved when he spoke, the inquisitive arch of his right brow. She'd loved the feel of her hand in his. He'd made her feel safe.

At first.

Unfortunately, as her pregnancy had progressed and her condition had become more fragile, he hadn't been able to cope. Instead of taking care of her, assuring her that everything would be okay, she had been the one constantly soothing his anxieties and fears.

She'd convinced herself that once the boys were born, things would go back to normal. But even after the twins were home from the hospital and out of danger, Jeremy's temperament had continued to deteriorate until she'd felt as if she had three children and no husband. Some days he hadn't even gotten out of bed, and he'd begun to resent the twins for taking up all of her time. He'd even accused her of loving the children more than she loved him.

She'd kept waiting for things to change, for him to go back to being the sweet, sensitive and attentive man she'd married. How could she have known that that man had never existed?

"If you hadn't talked to Jeremy in so long, how did you know he'd died?" she asked Jason.

"I got a call from my attorney. For the first time in five years his allowance went untouched for over a month. I knew something had to be wrong."

Holly's jaw fell and her heart broke all over again. "He had an allowance?"

"You didn't know," he said, and she shook her head, feeling sick all the way to her soul.

She was beginning to wonder if Jeremy had told her the truth about anything.

"I apologize if I'm getting too personal," Jason said. "But where did you think the money was coming from? Did he have a job?"

"He told me that he had been in a terrible car accident when he was a teenager that permanently damaged his back. He claimed the money was from a lawsuit settlement. But there was no accident, was there? And no settlement."

Jason actually cringed, as if it pained him to admit the truth. "Not that I know of."

Had any of it been real? Had Jeremy honestly loved her and the boys? Had he even been capable of that kind of love?

"Will you be staying here, in the city?" Jason asked.

The idea of how and where she would find an affordable apartment without a job or money filled her heart with dread. "I—I don't know. Yet."

"I'd like the chance to get to know my nephews. They are the only family I have left."

"Of course. I would love that. I'm just… Suffice it to say that things are a little up in the air right now. But as soon as we're settled I'll let you know."

Though she tried to put on a good face, Jason's look of skepticism said he wasn't buying it. He studied her with the same stormy blue eyes as his brother. So alike, yet not. "You have nowhere to go, do you?"

She squared her shoulders and lifted her chin, saying with a confidence she was nowhere close to feeling, "I'll find something."

"You mentioned selling the ring. Do you have any other resources? Was there life insurance?"

If only. But that wasn't his problem. "We'll get by."

"I'll take that as a no." He sighed and shook his head, mumbling under his breath. "He left you with nothing, didn't he?"

No, he'd left her with something. A big old pile of debt and two very hungry mouths to feed. She lowered her gaze, clasping her hands in her lap so he wouldn't see that they were trembling. "We'll manage."

"How?"

She blinked. "Excuse me?"

"How will you manage? What's your plan?"

Good question. "Well… I haven't figured *everything* out yet, but I will."

When she'd met Jeremy she had just moved to New York and had been staying with the brother of a friend back home in Florida, where she'd been raised. At the time, meeting Jeremy had felt like destiny. But now, with her life in shambles, if it wasn't for her precious boys, she might have wished she'd never met him.

Though her tone conveyed the utmost confidence, Holly's eyes told an entirely different tale. Jason could see that deep down she was scared—terrified even—at the prospect of supporting herself and his nephews. But she was clearly in no position to support herself, much less twin infants. And he was in the perfect position to help her. If she would only let him.

His biggest hurdle would be her pride, which she seemed to possess in excess. But he had learned long ago that there was a very fine line between pride and irresponsibility.

He heard the wail of an infant and realized it was coming from the baby monitor on the coffee table. Then a pair of wails, like baby stereo.

Holly sighed, looking exhausted and overwhelmed, and Jason wondered how long it had been since she'd had a decent night's sleep. He could only imagine how difficult life had been for her lately, being a recent widow with twins. And then along he'd come to tell her that everything she knew about her husband was a lie.

Talk about rubbing salt in the wound.

"Would you like to meet your nephews?" she asked.

His heart jumped in his chest at the prospect of meeting twins who were now his only family. "Of course I would."

She pushed herself up from the couch, wobbling slightly before she caught her balance. She flashed him a weak smile and said, "Still a little woozy, I guess."

And who could blame her? He rose, prepared to catch her if she fell over or, God forbid, lost consciousness again, as he didn't have the first clue what to do with a screaming infant. Let alone two screaming infants. He followed closely behind her, and as she opened the bedroom door, it was obvious that both his nephews had healthy lungs. He never would have imagined that anything so small could make such a racket.

She switched on the light and Jason held his breath as he peeked over her shoulder into the cribs at his nephews. There was no doubt they took after his side of the family. It was like looking at photos of himself and his brother at that age.

Holly lifted one wailing infant and then turned to

Jason and held the little boy out to him. "Jason, meet Devon," she said.

Jason just stood there, unsure of what to do.

"He won't bite," Holly said.

Jason took the infant under the arms and he quieted instantly. He looked so tiny and fragile wrapped in Jason's big hands, his blue eyes wide. And he hardly weighed anything.

"This little complainer is Marshall," she said, lifting him from the other crib. She propped him on her shoulder and patted his back, which did nothing to stop his wailing. He must have been the feistier of the two.

"Marshall was our grandfather's name," Jason told her.

Holly turned to him, saw the way he was holding her son and smiled. "You know, he won't break."

"I've never held a child this small," Jason admitted, feeling completely out of his element. In business he'd dealt with some of the most powerful people in the country, yet he had no idea what to do with this tiny, harmless human being. "He looks so fragile. What if I drop him?"

"You won't," she said, and he hoped her confidence wasn't misplaced.

Noting the way Holly held Marshall over her shoulder, he set Devon against his chest, placing one hand under his diapered behind and the other on his back to steady him. But he realized as Devon lifted his little head off Jason's shoulder to stare at him, blue eyes wide and inquisitive, he wasn't as fragile as he looked.

Jason watched Holly as she laid Marshall, who was still howling, on the changing table and deftly changed his diaper, cooing and talking to him in a quiet, soothing voice, her smile so full of love and affection Jason kind of wished she would smile at him that way.

She's your sister-in-law, he reminded himself. But damn, she was pretty. In an unspoiled, wholesome way.

Women, as he saw it, were split between two categories. There were the ones who wanted the traditional life of marriage and babies, and those who balked at the mention of commitment. He preferred the latter. For some people, marriage and family just weren't in the cards.

Holly turned to Jason, held out her son and said, "Switch."

It was an awkward handover, and Marshall hollered the entire time Jason held him. It was hard not to take it personally.

"Would you like to help me feed them?"

"I don't know how."

"There's nothing to it," she assured him with a smile. After all she had been through, the fact that she still could smile was remarkable.

Feeling completely out of his element, Jason sat on the couch while his nephew sucked hungrily on a bottle and stared up at him.

Although not by choice, children had never been a part of his life plan, so he usually did what he could to avoid them. But if he was going to be a good uncle, he supposed he should at least try to learn to care for them. If, God forbid, something were to happen to Holly, they would be his sole responsibility. And then, if something were to happen to him, if his illness were to return, who would take them?

The idea was both humbling and terrifying.

This was the absolute last place he had expected to end up when he'd left home today.

Their bottoms dry and their bellies full, the boys fell sound sleep, and Jason helped her put them in their cribs.

"How often do you have to do that?" he asked Holly as she stood at the sink rinsing the empty bottles.

"Every three hours. Sometimes more, sometimes less. They've never slept more than a four-hour stretch."

That would be an average of eight times a day. Two babies, all by herself.

He had a sudden newfound respect for single mothers.

"How do you manage it alone?"

Her tone nonchalant, she said, "I've learned to multitask."

He had the feeling it was a bit more complicated than that. How was she supposed to get a job with the boys to care for? Day care, he supposed. Call him old-fashioned, but he wanted to see his nephews raised by their mother, the way he and his brother had been raised by theirs. He had nothing but fond memories of his early childhood. Life had been close to perfect back then.

Until it hadn't been anymore.

She finished the bottles and wiped her hands on a dish towel. "Thanks for the help."

"Anytime," he said, and he meant it. "In fact, I'll be back in the city next week and I was hoping I could spend some time with the boys."

"You don't live in New York?"

"After our father died I moved upstate." The lake house had been in their family for generations and had been his favorite retreat as a child.

"Jeremy used to talk about us moving upstate, getting a house in a small town. A fixer-upper that we could make ours. With a big yard and a swing set for the boys. I can't help thinking that was probably a lie, too."

Sadly, it probably was. Jeremy had preferred the anonymity of living in a big city. Not to mention the ease with which he could support his drug habit. Something told Jason that wouldn't have changed.

Jason always had been the one who'd strived for a slower-paced lifestyle. Ten years of working for his father had landed him on the business fast track, but his heart had never really been in it. Only after his father's death had he started living the life he'd wanted.

"You and the boys should come and visit me," he told her, surprised and hopeful when her eyes lit.

"I'd like that. But are you sure you have the space? I don't want to put you out."

At first he thought she was joking, and then he remembered that she knew virtually nothing about their family. Or their finances. Maybe for right now it would be better if he didn't bring up the fact that her sons stood to inherit millions someday. It might be too much to take all in one night. And though Jeremy had been disinherited years ago, he would see that Holly and the boys were well cared for.

"I have space," he assured her. Maybe once he got her there, once she saw how much room he had and how good life would be there for them, he could convince her to stay, giving him the chance to right the last wrong his brother would ever commit. He owed it to his nephews.

And to himself.

Three

Jason sat at the bar of The Trapper Tavern, the town watering hole, nursing an imported beer with his best friend and attorney Lewis Pennington.

"Are you sure you can trust her?" Lewis asked him after he explained the situation with his sister-in-law and nephews. "I don't have to tell you the sort of people with whom your brother kept company. She could be conning you."

Jason didn't think so. "Lewis, she was so freaked out she actually fainted when she saw me, and she seemed to genuinely have no clue who Jeremy really was."

"Or she's as good an actor as your brother."

"Or she's an innocent victim."

"With your flesh and blood involved, is that a chance you really want to take?"

Of course not. The day his brother died was the day the twins' happiness and well-being had become Jason's responsibility. "That's why, when she's here, I'm going to ask her to stay with me. Until she's back on her feet financially."

He'd left Holly his phone number and told her to call if she needed anything. She'd called the next morning sounding tired and exasperated, asking to take him up on his offer to visit, saying she needed a few days away from the city. In the background he could hear his nephews howling. He admired the fact that she wasn't afraid to admit she needed help. And he was more than happy to supply it. That and so much more.

"My point is that you know nothing about this woman," Lewis said. "Don't let the fact that she's the mother of your nephews cloud your judgment."

"With a brother like Jeremy, I've learned to be a pretty good judge of character."

"Maybe so, but I'd hide the good china, just in case."

Jason shot him a look.

"At least let me run a background check, search for a criminal history."

"If you insist, but I doubt you'll find anything."

"When is her train due in?"

Jason glanced at his watch. "An hour."

He'd offered to drive to the city and pick up her and the boys at her apartment, but she'd insisted they take the train. And when he'd tried to talk her out of it, she'd only dug her heels in deeper. Though he barely knew her, he could see that persuading her to do something she didn't want to do was going to be difficult, if not impossible.

"If she's so destitute, why not just pay her debt and set her up in her own place in town? What woman wouldn't go for that?"

The kind who was too proud for her own good. And

as much as it annoyed him, he couldn't help but respect that. "I offered to pay all the debt Jeremy left her with and help her get a fresh start."

"And?"

He took a long swallow of his beer, then set the bottle down on the bar. "She wouldn't take a penny."

Lewis's brows rose in surprise. "Seriously?"

"She wouldn't budge."

"She's independent?"

That was putting it mildly. "You have no idea."

"Attractive?"

Immensely. "That's irrelevant."

Lewis grinned. "Are you attracted to her?"

Hell yes, he was. Who wouldn't be? "She's my sister-in-law. My feelings are irrelevant."

"Not if you plan to live under the same roof with her. Feelings have a way of happening whether we want them to or not."

"My only concern is for my nephews."

"What if you ask her to stay with you and she refuses?"

"Obviously I can't force her."

"That's not necessarily true."

Jason frowned. "What do you mean?"

"You have leverage."

"Leverage?"

"Your nephews. You could threaten to sue her for custody."

"On what grounds? She seems perfectly competent to me." Not to mention the damage it would cause the twins, first losing their father, then being ripped away from their mother.

"If she's as destitute as you claim, the last thing she'll

want is a legal battle. The threat of one could make her more likely to cooperate."

Or put her right over the edge. He did worry that getting her cooperation would be difficult, but he couldn't imagine ever taking it to that extreme. However, if there was any validity to Lewis's suspicions, Jason could be downright ruthless if it meant keeping his nephews safe. But there was no need to jump the gun. Unlike his father, who had been quick to judge and considered anyone he didn't know well a potential threat, Jason preferred to grant people the benefit of the doubt. Innocent until proven guilty. But he knew he could never convince Lewis that she was telling the truth, so he didn't even try.

"How is Miranda?" he asked his friend.

Lewis sighed and rolled his eyes. "All whacked out on hormones again."

Lewis and his wife had been trying unsuccessfully to conceive a baby over the course of their three-year marriage. They had tried every method, be it Western medicine or holistic, with no success. They were now on their third IVF attempt in nine months, and it had been emotionally taxing on them both. Though more so on Miranda, Jason imagined. Lewis had a teenage son from a former relationship, someone to carry on his legacy.

Jason found it ironic that Jeremy, who'd lacked the integrity to care for his own sons, had had no problem at all conceiving a child, while good people such as Lewis and Miranda, who had everything to offer a son or daughter, were helpless to make it happen.

"When is the next procedure?" Jason asked.

"Next Friday," Lewis said, eyes on the thirty-year-old scotch that he swirled in his glass. "And regardless of the outcome, it will be our last."

"What?" Jason set down his bottle a little harder than he'd meant to. "You're just going to give up?"

"After three years the perpetual disappointment is taking a toll on us both. We've begun to look into foreign adoption instead."

"Another time-consuming process," Jason said and Lewis nodded.

"But when we're approved, at least there will be a light at the end of the tunnel."

"Have you considered a surrogate?"

"Only to have her change her mind after the baby is born? It would destroy Miranda."

Yes, it probably would. "I'm sorry, Lewis. I wish there was something I could do."

"We'll get through this."

Jason didn't envy their situation. Though it had taken years of introspection and soul searching, he'd come to terms with the fact that he would never have a family of his own. Now it would seem he'd earned one by default.

Longest. Trip. Ever.

Despite Holly's hope that the twins would sleep most of the five-hour train ride, they had fussed and complained, sleeping in fits and bursts, and generally making a nuisance of themselves. By the time Holly got them in the stroller and ready to depart the train, she'd expended the last of her energy and was running on pure adrenaline, wishing she had taken Jason up on his offer to give them a ride. But now as she sat in Jason's black luxury SUV, the boys buckled safely in the back, that adrenaline was wearing thin.

After today it was abundantly clear that if Holly was

going to make it as a single mom of twins, she was going to have to sock away her pride and learn to accept help a little more often. For the twins' sake. They were a handful now, but what about when they began to crawl and walk and get into things? Just the idea made her weary. She knew she should be in New York looking for a job and a place to live, and taking this vacation was irresponsible and selfish, but her sanity depended on it.

While Jason loaded their bags in the back, she looked over her shoulder into the backseat, peering into the boy's car seats. They were both out cold. She would have wept with relief, but she didn't have the energy.

"Rough trip?" Jason asked as he opened the driver's side door and climbed in, flashing her a smile. One she felt from the ends of her hair to the tips of her toes and everywhere in between.

Whoa. Where the heck had that come from? She turned away, pretending to look out the window at the station, hoping he wouldn't notice her conspicuously rosy cheeks. It wasn't helping matters that he smelled absolutely delicious, like some manly musk drifting on a warm spring breeze.

She tried to fight it, but it was hopeless. Ribbons of heat twisted through her veins, making her skin flush. Making her feel restless and aroused.

In all the time she had been with Jeremy, Holly had never experienced this intense physical reaction from a simple smile. To be fair, she hadn't had sex in over six months, though it felt more like a year. Or five.

Her cheeks burned hotter. She really shouldn't be thinking about sex right now. But the harder she tried not to think about it, the further her mind strayed.

"Everyone buckled and ready to go?" Jason asked her as the engine roared to life. She could feel his eyes on her; she had no choice but to face him. The alternative was to act rudely.

Willing away the heat rushing to her face, she turned to him, her gaze instantly locking on his stormy eyes. Though it was wildly bizarre, she didn't look at Jason and see Jeremy anymore. They may have been identical in looks, but his personality and disposition set Jason apart from his brother.

His brow wrinkled. "Are you feeling okay? You're flushed."

Aw, hell. "I'm fine. Really. Just tired."

Concern etching the corners of his eyes, Jason reached up to touch her burning hot cheek with his cool, surprisingly rough fingers, then frowned and pressed the back of his hand to her forehead, the way her mom had when Holly was a little girl. "You're warm."

No kidding. She was surprised her face hadn't melted off. And the fact that he kept touching her wasn't helping matters.

He was dressed much more casually today, in dark slacks and a white polo shirt that contrasted sharply with his deeply tanned face. Considering it was only the first week of June, she was guessing he spent a considerable amount of time outdoors. If she lived near a lake, she probably would, too. As a young teen one of her favorite pastimes had been going fishing with her foster dad and siblings. She had always hoped someday she would be able to share those experiences with her own children.

"We have to go through town to get to my place," Jason told her as he pulled out of the lot. "Do you need to stop for anything or would you prefer to go straight to the house?"

"House, please. How far is it from town?"

"Ten minutes, give or take. I'm on the far side of the lake."

Trapper Cove, which was indeed tucked back into a cove off Trapper Lake, was just as she always pictured a small upstate New York town to look. Quaint and clean and undeniably upscale. She rolled her window down and took a deep breath of fresh lake air. So different from the city.

As they headed down Main Street into the heart of the town, Jason gave her a brief history lesson on the various shops and businesses. They passed a marina and boat launch, and a members' only yacht club. On the water she counted at least a dozen of what her foster brother, Tyler, would have called "big ass" boats. He also would have commented on the luxury import cars lining the pristine streets. She wondered if the area had been this posh when Jason and Jeremy were kids. When Jeremy supposedly had been living on the streets and begging for food.

Just thinking his name made her heart hurt. It still astounded her how many lies he'd told, and how she had been married to a man she didn't even know. Looking back, which she had been doing an awful lot since she'd met Jason, she realized that life with Jeremy had never been a fantastic love story. They'd met and started to date, and three months later she'd found herself pregnant. When Jeremy had insisted on marrying her she'd thought the true love part would come later, when they got to know one another better. Clearly she had been wrong. She hadn't known him at all. The man she thought she'd fallen in love with didn't even exist.

Never in her life had she felt so betrayed.

As they drove slowly through the center of town,

people stopped to wave and shout hello to Jason, and she received more than a few curious glances.

"It's a beautiful town," she told him. "You seem to know a lot about it. And a lot of people."

"Jeremy and I spent every summer here as kids with our mom and grandparents. Our dad came up on weekends when he could get away from work."

She couldn't imagine a more ideal setting to spend her summers. Or her winters. Or springs and falls, as well. "So you live here year round now?"

"I do."

"Are you close to the lake?"

"About as close as you can get without living in a house boat."

She blinked with surprise. "You live *on* the lake?"

"Straight across from town."

She peered out the car window across the lake. She could barely make out the silhouette of homes tucked back against the thick forest bordering the shore; at this distance she could see very little detail. Among them, nearly hidden behind a row of towering pine trees, stood what appeared to be some sort of enormous and rustic-looking wood structure. Maybe a hotel or hunting lodge. It was too huge to be someone's home.

"Can you see your house from here?" she asked him, as they passed the Trapper Drugstore and The Trapper Inn. Beside that sat the Trapper Tavern.

"Barely," he said. "I'll point it out to you the next time we're in town."

He left Main Street and the town behind and turned onto a densely wooded two-lane road that circled the lake. Mottled sunshine danced across the windshield through breaks in the trees, and every so often she could see snippets of clear blue lake. The earthy scents of the forest filled the car. It was so dark and quiet and peaceful. She closed her eyes and breathed in deep, and like magic she could feel the knots in her muscles releasing, her frayed nerves mending. For the first time since Jeremy died she was giving herself permission to relax.

It felt strange, but in a good way.

After several minutes Jason steered the vehicle down a long and bumpy dirt road. "There's something you don't see in the city," Jason said, pointing to a family of deer foraging just off the road. They were almost close enough to reach out the car window and touch.

The trees opened up to a small clearing, and towering over them stood what she had assumed was a lodge, so deeply tucked into the surrounding forest, the dark wood exterior seemed to blend in with the vegetation. But as they pulled up to the front entrance, she could see that this was no lodge. This was a house. A really *huge* house.

She took a deep breath and willed herself not to freak out. She should have known. Most people of modest means did not spend their summers at the lake house. That in itself should have been her first clue that Jason's family was well-to-do. But she never would have guessed that they had done this well.

The summers that Jeremy had claimed he'd spent living on the street, begging for food, he'd actually been here, in a *mansion*?

Holly felt sick all the way to her bones. Any lingering traces of love or respect for her dead husband fizzled away. She had never been more deeply saddened or utterly disappointed in anyone.

Jason parked close to the door, cut the engine and turned to her, watching expectantly when he said, "Home sweet home."

Four

Holly peered out the car window, craning to see way, way, way up three floors of towering wood beams and glass. She had never seen a house with so many huge windows. The view from inside had to be incredible. The house somehow managed to look traditional and modern at the same time.

And here she had worried that being in close quarters with her brother-in-law might be awkward. "I guess you weren't exaggerating when you said you had room for us."

Jason winced a little. "It wasn't my intention to blind-side you."

"You just didn't want to overwhelm me. I get it."

"You're not angry?"

She smiled and shook her head. How could she be? His intentions were good and his heart in the right place, and in her opinion that was all that mattered.

Besides, to learn the depth of Jeremy's lies in one huge dose would have been too much to bear in her fragile state. Spoon-feeding her small bites of the truth made it a little easier to digest.

The front door opened and an older couple stepped outside. After a brief moment of confusion, Holly realized that they must work for Jason. A dwelling this enormous would obviously require a staff.

They met her at the car door as she climbed out.

"You must be Holly," the woman said with a distinct New England accent, taking Holly's hand and pumping it enthusiastically. "We're so pleased to finally meet you."

"Holly, this is Faye and George Henderson," Jason told her.

If she had to guess, Holly would put the couple somewhere in their early to mid-sixties. "It's so nice to meet you both."

"Aye-yup," George said in a voice as rough and craggy as his weathered face. He was a huge man, even taller than Jason and impressively muscular for someone of his advanced age.

"Now let me see those little angels I've heard so much about," Faye said, rubbing her palms together, eyes sparkling. She was small in stature, but there was a sturdiness about her that said she wasn't afraid of hard work.

Jason opened the car door and Faye peered inside, gasping softly, tears welling in her eyes. "Oh, Holly, they're beautiful. Your parents would have been so proud, Jason. Wouldn't they, George?"

George peered over his wife's shoulder into the backseat. "Aye-yup. They surely would."

"Let's get Holly settled into her room," Jason said.

He and Faye helped with the boys, who didn't even rouse, while George took care of the bags. The interior of the house was open concept, and with all of those enormous windows, felt like an extension of the forest. With its massive stone fireplace and overstuffed furniture, the decor was an eclectic cross of country cottage and shabby chic. In the center of the first floor stood a staircase like she'd never seen before. At least five feet wide, with lacquered tree branch banisters, it wound its way up to the second floor. Holly followed Jason up, her legs feeling like limp noodles.

At the top was a large, open area with more overstuffed, comfortable looking furniture, its walls lined floor-to-the ceiling with richly stained bookcases, their shelves sagging under the weight of volumes and volumes of books. She had never seen so many outside of a library.

Another set of those enormous windows boasted a breathtaking view of the lake, and below, off the back of the house, a multi-level deck.

To the left was a hallway that led to the bedrooms and on the opposite side, another smaller set of stairs.

"This is incredible," she told Jason, who had lugged Devon, still sound asleep in his car seat, and the diaper bag up the stairs. "I can understand why you wanted to stay here instead of the city."

"I've always considered this my true home," he said, leading her down the short hallway to the bedrooms. As she peered in through each doorway, she could see that the rooms were spacious and tastefully decorated. Warm and homey and comfortable, but in a refined, upscale way.

"Which room is yours?" she asked, and the idea of

him sleeping just a door or two away made her heart jump in her chest. But he pointed up, to the ceiling.

"I'm upstairs in the loft."

Wow. *Another* floor? This was a whole lot of house for one guy.

"Here's the nursery," he said, shouldering the door open.

Nursery? Why would a single guy need a nursery?

The truth was she knew very little about his life. She knew he'd never been married and had no children. Whether that was by choice or circumstance she didn't know. But she could see that the furnishings in the nursery were far too modern and pristine to be anything but brand-new.

"You bought furniture," she said, and from the looks of it, every other baby accessory that she might possibly need. And there were two of everything. Two cribs, two chests of drawers. Even two closets. And lots of toys. A child would want for nothing in this room. "It's perfect."

He set the car seat on the floor next to one of the cribs. "I'd like to take credit, but Faye is the genius behind this. I didn't have a clue what you would need."

"It was nothing," Faye said, waving away the compliment with a flick of her wrist as she crouched down to unbuckle Marshall from his car seat.

"You did all this for one little visit?" Holly asked Jason.

He turned to her. "The first visit of many, I'm hoping."

He smiled, and something in his eyes, in the way he looked at her, made her feel all warm and gooey inside. They stood that way for several seconds, just looking at each other, and though it sounded silly even to herself, she could swear that for an instant time stood still.

"Why don't you show Holly to her room while I tend to the boys?" Faye said, lifting a passed out Marshall from his car seat and onto her shoulder.

Holly tore her gaze away from Jason. "I can get them."

"Nonsense," Faye said. "You're obviously exhausted. You get yourself settled while I take care of these little angels."

If she had been on the train with them, she might not be so quick to call them angels.

Holly started to follow Jason out, but hesitated at the door, looking back at her sons. Since they'd come home from the hospital they had barely been out of her sight. And though they were perfectly healthy now and growing like weeds, leaving them in someone else's care made her palms sweat.

"You go on along," Faye said with an understanding smile. "They'll be fine. I practically raised Jason and Jeremy."

Learn to accept help, she chanted, and forced herself to say, "Okay, thank you."

Her room was the next one over. It was enormous, with its own full bathroom and walk-in closet. The furniture was knotty pine, and the king-size bed was draped with a huge, hand-sewn quilt.

"I think this room alone is bigger than my entire apartment," she told Jason. "It's a beautiful house. Thank you for letting us visit."

"You're welcome anytime." He smiled and she got that warm squishy feeling again, as if her insides had started to melt and were getting all mixed together. It was difficult to look at him without getting caught up in the blue of his eyes. She couldn't recall Jeremy's eyes ever captivating her this way.

She was just tired. And confused. Things would be clearer after she'd had a few hours of sleep. She hoped.

Jason must have read her mind. "Would you like to lie down for a while?"

Oh, would she ever. She crossed to the bed and ran her hand over the quilt. It was so pretty that she was afraid she might damage it. "It will be nice sleeping in a real bed again. An air mattress just isn't the same."

He looked confused. "You don't have a bed?"

"I do, but that was where…you know, I found him."

He winced a little. "Sorry, I didn't realize."

"And there was no way you could have known."

"I guess we haven't really talked about that," he said.

No, but they probably should, just to get it out of the way. She sat on the edge of the bed. "There isn't much to tell, really. When I first walked in I thought he was just taking a nap. As I got closer to the bed I could sense that something was wrong. Then I…" She stopped to swallow the lump in her throat. "He was cold to the touch, so I knew it had been awhile…"

He winced again, as if hearing the events of his brother's death pained him. And why wouldn't that be the case? Despite Jeremy's shortcomings, they were still twin brothers, identical in almost every way.

"I'm sorry," Jason said. "I didn't mean to dredge that up."

Not a day passed—hell, not even an hour—when she didn't see in her mind the image of her husband lying there. Nothing he could have done, no lie he could have told, would make her wish him dead. And though his death still upset her, her feelings had changed so drastically since she'd learned the truth. Those first few weeks had been torture, and she had missed him so terribly, but then, in a small way, she had begun to feel almost relieved. Not that he was dead, but that she would no longer have to deal with his erratic mood swings.

"I knew," Jason said, sitting down on the bed beside her. "I could *feel* that something was wrong, if that makes any sense."

"That's not unusual for twins, is it?"

"I could *always* feel his presence. Even when we were thousands of miles apart. Then he was just… gone." He turned to look at her and there was so much sadness in his eyes she wanted to hug him, but that felt like crossing a line.

"Now it feels as though a part of me is missing. Like it's just, if you'll pardon the expression, *dead space*."

"I can't even imagine being that close to another person."

"It's the sort of thing you don't think about, or even notice, until it's not there anymore."

"I'm so sorry," she said, laying a hand on his arm. He glanced at her hand, then up at her face, and there was a look in his eyes like…well, she couldn't say for sure what sort of look it was, but she knew that it made her insides feel funny.

"The twins are asleep," Faye said as she stepped into the room. Holly snatched her hand from Jason's arm, feeling a bit as if they'd been caught doing something naughty. Which they hadn't been. At all. Still she felt compelled to explain. But she didn't.

"Thank you," Holly said and left it at that.

"Is there anything I can do for you before I start dinner?" Faye asked. "Anything you need?"

"Just a nap."

Faye smiled. "Make it a quick one. Dinner is in one hour."

When she was gone, Holly told Jason, "She's so nice."

"She's thrilled to have you here. So is George. He's just not as likely to show it."

He did look like the strong silent type, a lot like her foster dad had been. A gentle giant. Holly sighed and rubbed her temples, longing for rest, but she was too wired to sleep.

"Headache?" Jason asked her, and she nodded. "I think there's a bottle of pain reliever in the bathroom. Let me go look."

"I can—" Before she could offer to do it herself he was halfway to the bathroom. "—Or not."

Just to test out the bed, Holly swung her legs around and lay down, her head sinking into the pillow.

Oh. My. God. She'd never been on a mattress so comfortable. It was like a little slice of heaven. She dared to close her eyes for just a second, knowing she should check on the boys. And that was the last thing she remembered.

Bottle of ibuprofen and a glass of water in hand, Jason walked back into the bedroom, but it was too late. Holly was out cold and snoring softly. She was so pretty and wholesome-looking that it damn near knocked his socks off. And sweet. Far too sweet and earnest for her own good. Her marriage to Jeremy was proof of that. It was a relief to know that with him, she and his nephews would be safe and well taken care of.

He set the bottle and glass on the table beside the bed in case she woke and needed them. He took a quick peek in the nursery, but didn't go in. Both boys seemed to be sleeping soundly, and he didn't want to risk waking them.

His phone started to ring and he quickly stepped into the hallway. It was Lewis.

"I did the background check."

That was quick. He wondered if that was a good or bad thing. "And?"

"She is who she says she is. She has no criminal record. Hell, as far as I can tell she's never had so much as a speeding ticket."

Jason had expected as much, but it was a relief to know for sure.

"I also looked into her financial status."

Now this was the part Jason wanted to hear. *"And?"*

"It's bad."

His gut clenched. "How bad?"

"Credit cards, personal loans, student loans. And they're all in default. Her credit rating is in the toilet."

Jason cursed. "How much in total."

Lewis told him the sum and Jason cursed again. *Jesus, Jeremy, why? Why her?*

Jason knew what he had to do, and he wouldn't be satisfied, wouldn't be able to sleep at night, until he made this right. "Pay it off. All of it."

"I thought she didn't want you to do that."

"I don't care. Just take care of it."

"If that's what you really want."

"It is."

He hung up and headed downstairs to talk to Faye. He found her in the kitchen waiting for him. She stood with her arms crossed, foot tapping, wearing her exactly-what-do-you-think-you're-doing-mister face. She may have been a small woman, but she was a force to be reckoned with.

And though he had a pretty good idea why she was in such a snit, he shrugged and said, *"What?"*

"You know that I don't like to meddle—"

He laughed. "Yes, you do."

Since his mother had passed away, Faye had taken it upon herself to, as she put it, keep Jason honest. Not that it was ever necessary, as he was the twin who never went against the grain. He did exactly what was expected of him without fail, always going above and beyond the call of duty. It was his curse. He was the "good" twin. And now, the *only* twin. It was a blessing that his parents hadn't lived to see Jeremy completely self-destruct. It would have devastated their mother. She had blamed herself for Jeremy's behavior. Thought it was as much Jason's fault. More so, even.

"She's adorable," Faye said. "And sweet."

Yes, she was. Too adorable and sweet for someone like him. "You say that as if it's a bad thing. Would you prefer that she be unattractive and incorrigible?"

Faye gave him another look. "And obviously very vulnerable."

"And you think I would take advantage of that?"

"Not on purpose."

"I only want to help her, to make up for what Jeremy did to her. Her and the boys."

Faye wasn't buying it. "That's it, huh?"

"Why is that so difficult to believe?"

"Because I saw the way you were looking at her."

"No crime in looking." Faye knew he didn't do commitment. That he could never have a family of his own. Holly had already been taken advantage of by one Cavanaugh. He would never do anything to hurt her. At least, not intentionally.

Faye's deep frown said she didn't like his answer. "Are you still going to ask her to stay?"

"She has nowhere else to go. Jeremy put her so far into debt she'll never dig herself out."

Faye frowned. "How much did he take her for?"

Jason told her and Faye gasped, holding a hand to her bosom. "Oh, good lord. That poor thing."

"Don't worry. I'm taking care of it. She needs help, even if she won't admit it. My number one priority is the twins and seeing that they're raised properly. Someday my entire fortune will be theirs. They need to be prepared if they're going to carry on the Cavanaugh dynasty responsibly. They need the proper breeding and a top-notch education. I can provide that. Not to mention a stable and substance-free environment to raise them in. I refuse to let them turn out like their father."

Looking indignant, she said, "You're not suggesting that Holly isn't fit to be a parent because she doesn't have the right breeding."

He sighed. "Call it what you will. Wealth is a huge responsibility and at times a terrible burden. And as we've learned with Jeremy, it can easily be mismanaged. I want them to be prepared for whatever life throws at them."

"As long as you remember that Holly is their parent and no decisions can be made without her approval."

"I realize that." Of course he would never try to undermine her authority, but he also knew what was best for his nephews, and he would make Holly see that.

Five

Holly woke slowly from her nap, feeling so cozy and comfortable on the firm mattress that she could easily have drifted back off to sleep. She almost did, but snapped herself awake. The boys would be waking soon to be fed and she should think about eating something herself. If she lost any more weight she was going to look like a skeleton. She reached for her phone, and checked the time. 8:07 p.m. Well, she'd probably missed dinner, but that was okay. Faye struck her as the type who might keep a plate of leftovers warm.

Holly sat up and blinked herself awake, surprised by how well-rested she felt after only a few hours of sleep. She got up and walked to the window. The water was clear and calm and—

Hold on. Where the heck did all the boats go? And why was the sun on the wrong side of the lake?

She looked at her phone again and realized it wasn't

eight in the evening. It was morning, and she had slept *all night*!

The air whooshed from her lungs as if she'd been punched in the stomach. She rushed to the door and yanked it open, startling Jason, who was on the other side, fist raised, about to knock.

"Well, good morning. Faye sent me up to tell you that breakfast..." He trailed off, concern in his eyes. "You look like you just saw a ghost."

Nope, just hyperventilating. "Where are the boys?"

"In the kitchen with Faye."

"They're okay?"

Jason looked confused, as if he thought she might be a little loony. "Of course they are."

She was so relieved she had to grab the door frame to keep her knees from buckling.

"What did you think I would do, sell them on the black market?"

She *hadn't been* thinking, that was the problem. She'd just reacted. "No, of course not. It's just that we haven't been apart much since they came home from the hospital. They are almost never out of my sight. I only just started sleeping in the living room instead of on their bedroom floor."

"Take a deep, slow breath," he said.

She took three, then another, until she could feel the knots in her stomach unwinding, her pulse slowing. This was not the way she had hoped to start her morning. This trip was supposed to be fun and relaxing. They were supposed to be getting to know one another.

"Better?" he asked.

She nodded, feeling steadier. And pretty darned ridiculous for overreacting. "I panicked. I'm sorry. I didn't mean to be so rude."

"You weren't rude."

"It's just that they were so fragile when they were born, and though I know that now they're just as healthy as any other child their age, I always feel as if I'm waiting for the other shoe to fall."

"Holly?"

She looked up at him. She couldn't look his way without getting caught up in those ocean-blue irises. And the way he said her name made her insides feel warm and soft.

He laid his hands on her shoulders, giving them a reassuring squeeze. "You're safe here. I'm not going to let anything happen to you or the boys. I give you my word."

She believed him.

She barely knew this man, but she knew in her heart that he meant every word he said. And she was rational enough now to realize how nice his hands felt on her shoulders. A little *too* nice, in fact. There was nothing rational about *that*.

"You all right?" he asked, his hands slipping lower, to the tops of her arms.

More like confused. He was standing really close, and he smelled so good. It would be so easy to reach out and touch him…

No, she really shouldn't do that.

"I'm fine. Just a little disoriented."

"You missed dinner last night. You must be starving."

"I am," she said.

He dropped his hands from her arms and she was both relieved and disappointed. And clearly not thinking straight.

As they stepped into the hall she could smell bacon and freshly brewed coffee.

"How does a walk around the property sound after breakfast?" he asked as she followed him down the stairs.

"I'd like that." God only knew she could use some fresh air.

"I thought that we could go into town this afternoon."

"I'd love to."

The kitchen was huge and outfitted with top-of-the-line appliances that any chef would drool over. Faye stood at the stove stirring what looked like scrambled eggs, Devon on her hip, while Marshall squealed happily and kicked his chubby little legs in his car seat on the kitchen table. Holly needn't have worried, they looked happy and perfectly content in Faye's care, which Holly was ashamed to admit had her feeling the tiniest bit jealous. She was used to doing everything on her own.

Faye smiled when she saw Holly. "Well good morning, sleepy head. Are you hungry?"

Her mother used to call her that, and to hear it again made her smile.

"Starved," she said, lifting Marshall into her arms for a snuggle, tickling him under his chubby chin. He giggled and kicked and fisted her hair in his soggy hands. It occurred to her just then that she hadn't brushed her hair, or her teeth for that matter, and if that wasn't bad enough, she was wearing last night's clothes. She sneaked a look at her reflection in the stainless steel refrigerator. Her ponytail was a bit askew, and her clothes were wrinkled. But it wasn't as if Jason hadn't already seen her at her worst.

His cell phone rang and he pulled it from his pants

pocket. He checked the display and frowned. "Excuse me. I have to take this."

When he was gone, Faye asked Holly, "How did you sleep?"

Holly tried to straighten her hair but Marshall kept grabbing at it. "Like the dead. I didn't even hear the boys wake up. I'm a little surprised that they slept all night."

"They didn't," Faye said. "They woke up around dinner time and had a bottle. Then Jason and I played with them for a while. They conked out around ten and slept until about 2:00 a.m."

"Why didn't you wake me?"

"Jason asked me not to. He said things have been rough for you and you needed rest. He's a good man, you know."

Holly hiked Marshall up over what used to be her hip, but now was just a knobby bone. "I've noticed."

"After what happened to you with Jeremy..." She shook her head, looking so sad. "I just want you to know that Jason isn't at all like his brother."

"I can see that."

"I wish you had known Jeremy when he was younger. He used to be the sweetest boy. I wish I knew what happened, why he changed the way he did." She held out a plate of bacon and offered Holly a slice. "You must be famished."

Holly took a piece and bit into it, her mouth watering. Bacon was one of those things that always tasted better when someone else made it. "It's delicious. Thank you."

"You're all skin and bones. We need to fatten you up."

She had always been naturally thin. She'd only gained twenty pounds when she was pregnant with the twins. But Faye was right: now she was *too* thin.

She finished that slice and reached for another, dodging Marshall's sticky hand. "Do you and George live here in the house?"

"We live in the caretakers' cottage," Faye said, gesturing out the window above the kitchen sink. Holly craned her neck to see. The small dwelling had the same dark wood exterior as the main house and was set back several hundred feet in the forest. It blended in so well with the surrounding vegetation that Holly hadn't even noticed it when they'd gotten to the house yesterday.

"How long have you lived there?"

"Since I married George. His father was the caretaker for years, and his father before that. It's a family tradition."

Since being orphaned Holly missed out on family traditions, though her foster parents had done their best to give her a somewhat normal childhood. But without a real family it had never been the same. "And will your kids carry on the tradition?"

"Our only child died when he was very small."

Holly's heart ached just thinking about it. She couldn't imagine losing a child. Nor did she want to contemplate it. Some things were better left alone. "I'm so sorry."

"He was born with a genetic abnormality," Faye said. "He didn't even make it to his first birthday. His short life was filled with pain and suffering. My doctor warned us that if I were to have another child there was a chance it would suffer the same condition, so we decided it wasn't worth the risk. They knew so little about genetics back then."

The idea of never having children of her own hurt Holly's heart. She couldn't imagine life without her boys. "That must have been a difficult choice."

"I sank into deep depression for several months. But

then Jason and Jeremy were born and their mother was overwhelmed and needed my help. It wasn't the same as having my own children, but I loved them." Faye paused, looking sad. "If our boy had lived he would be forty this fall."

"What was his name?"

The memory made Faye smile. "His name was Travis. Travis George Henderson."

"It's a nice name."

"Travis was my father's name."

"Did you know when you were pregnant that anything was wrong?"

"We had no idea. And I had a perfectly normal pregnancy. But the minute he was born it was obvious that something was wrong. They couldn't get him to cry, and when he did it was so weak and raspy. Then I saw him. He wasn't normal, that much was obvious, but I thought he was the most beautiful baby I had ever seen. Jason's parents were so good to George and me. Though the Cavanaughs paid us generously, we were helping to support my parents and didn't have money for medical bills. Jason's father paid for Travis to see at least half a dozen specialists, but they all told us the same thing. He wouldn't live past his first birthday, and there wasn't anything anyone could do."

Holly had to swallow the huge lump in her throat so she could speak. "I'm so sorry, Faye."

"It's all a part of God's plan. And it was a long time ago. I just wanted you to know how good the Cavanaughs were to us. They took care of us, and Jason will do the same for you."

Whether Holly wanted him to or not, it would seem. If she'd known that he'd intended to let her sleep all night, she wouldn't have lain down for a nap. But she couldn't deny feeling the most rested she had since the twins were born. Maybe, just in this instance, he did know what was best for her. As long as he didn't make a habit of it.

Holly reached into her back pocket for her phone, realizing when she didn't feel it there that she must have left it upstairs. She'd called one of those credit counselors yesterday in the hopes that they might have some sort of financial solution for her and was waiting for a call back.

She asked Faye, "Can you watch them for a minute while I go grab my phone?"

"Of course, honey. Take your time."

Holly set Marshall back in his car seat and headed upstairs to her room. She found her phone on the bed where she must have dropped it. Aside from a dozen emails and Facebook notifications, there was a missed call from the financial people. She sat on the bed and listened to the voice mail they'd left. Then she listened again. Then once more to be sure she was hearing the agent correctly.

She stuffed her phone in her back pocket, but what she really wanted to do was chuck it at the wall. There was only one explanation for this. And though she rarely cursed, she shook her head and muttered, "Sonofabitch."

Jason waited until he was in his office with the door shut before he answered Lewis's call.

"It's done," he told Jason.

"You're sure you got everything."

"Down to that last penny."

"Thanks, Lewis."

"You may not be so grateful when she learns the

truth. How long do you think it will take her to figure it out?"

Not long enough, Jason was sure. And she would be
furious with him when she did. But she would get over
it. She would see that it was best for everyone.

"What was her reaction when she saw the house?"
Lewis asked him.

"She took it surprisingly well, all things considered."

"Have you asked her to stay?"

"No, not yet. I don't want to rush into anything or
overwhelm her. I want to give her time to settle in, to
feel comfortable here."

"I wouldn't wait too long. If she's as independent as
you claim—"

"Don't forget stubborn."

"Once she finds out you paid all her debt she's probably not going to be happy with you."

Lewis had a point. Maybe it would be better to ask
sooner rather than later.

"I almost forgot, Miranda wondered if you two—
sorry, make that *four*—would like to meet up for dinner
sometime. As you can imagine, she's anxious to meet
your nephews. And Holly."

"Sounds good."

"You don't want to ask Holly first?"

"It will do her good to get out with people."

"Okay, but do me a favor and don't tell her that I'm
the one responsible for her debt being paid off."

"You were operating under my instructions. She has
no one to blame but me."

"Yeah, but she might not see it that way. I'd rather
err on the side of caution if it's all the same to you."

Jason opened his mouth to reply but was interrupted

by very firm and insistent pounding on his office door. It was so loud that Lewis heard it over the phone.

"What the heck is that?" he asked Jason.

Before he could respond the door swung open and Holly barged right in uninvited. And she was not happy.

She glared at him, hands propped on what little she had in the way of hips, her ponytail still slightly askew, looking pretty damned adorable. "What the hell did you do?"

"I hate to say this," Lewis said, sounding amused. "But I think she knows."

"Astute observation," Jason said, his tone oozing sarcasm as he watched Holly stomp across the room to his desk. "I have to let you go."

Lewis chuckled. "I'll see you later. If you live that long."

"Thanks for the vote of confidence. I'll see you." Jason hung up, and in an attempt to diffuse the situation, gestured to the chair opposite his desk and said, "Have a seat."

She ignored the chair and propped both hands on the desktop, looking as if she might launch over it and strangle him to death. He had to bite down on his lip to keep from smiling. She looked about as threatening as a field mouse.

"I got an interesting message from my financial guy," she said.

He didn't realize she *had* a financial guy. That would have been good to know. "Did you?"

"Yes, he was supposed to help me figure out a way to consolidate all my debt. Needless to say he was a little confused when he discovered that I have no debt."

She was furious, and all Jason could think about was

pulling her down onto the surface of his desk and kissing that frown off those delicious lips.

Delicious lips? Seriously?

What was wrong with him? This was his sister-in-law he was lusting after. His brother's wife. It was the one thing he swore he wouldn't do. "It must be a relief not to have that hanging over your head," he said.

"Of course it is!" she said, bristling with outrage. "That's not the point."

He liked this bolder, saucier side. He wondered what else she was hiding under that demure outer shell. "Maybe it should be," he said, thinking how sexy she looked when she was angry. "Maybe you should try shelving the pride for five minutes and let someone help you."

"Is that what you think this is about? My *pride*?"

"It's not?"

She fisted her hands and he wondered if she would take a swing at him. "I asked you specifically not to get involved in my finances, and you said you wouldn't. Then you went behind my back and did it anyway."

He rose from his chair and walked around his desk. He thought about putting his hands on her shoulders the way he had that morning, just to calm her down, but she looked so beside herself with anger that he was afraid he might pull back two bloody stumps. "Holly, I only did what I knew was best for you. And the boys."

"What *you* knew was best?" She looked at him as though he was a moron. "Don't you get it? You *lied* to me, Jason. Right to my face. Without batting an eyelash."

She didn't come right out and compare him to his brother, but the implication was clear. The worst part was that she was right. No matter the reason for it, or his misguided good intentions, he *had* lied to her.

The women he usually kept company with would let a lie or two slide if it was materialistically advantageous. Which spoke volumes about his skewed attitude toward the opposite sex, he supposed. But Holly was unlike any woman he'd ever known. Strong and resilient and unwilling to compromise her principles, even if it meant putting herself through undue hardship.

And too damned sweet to be around someone like him.

"You're right," he said, angry with himself for thinking that after all she had been through she could be so easily manipulated. Or that he even had the right to try. Who was he to decide what was best for someone he'd known barely four days?

He'd always swore that no matter what his net worth, he wouldn't let money change him or give him a false sense of entitlement. He had officially become his own worst nightmare.

He really *was* a moron.

"I was wrong to go behind your back," he told her. "I hope you'll accept my apology and my promise that it will never happen again."

She took a few seconds to think about it, and he started to wonder if maybe he'd blown it, if she would pack up and leave and deny him the privilege of knowing his nephews. And could he blame her if she did?

"Apology accepted," she finally said.

She was giving him a second chance, and he'd be damned if he was going to screw it up. His relationship with his nephews depended on it. Besides, he could still take care of them, all three of them. He would just have to be a bit more subtle about it.

"Now that we have that settled, I have something that I need to say to you," Holly told him in an unsteady voice, as if she might burst out crying.

Uh-oh, this couldn't be good.

Making an effort not to wince and bracing himself for the worst, he said, "Let's have it."

"Thank you." She threw herself into his arms nearly knocking him backward. "Thank you so much, Jason."

Wait. Now she was thanking him? As long as he lived he would never understand women, and though he knew it was probably a bad idea, he slipped his arms around her, gently rubbing her back as he held her. Holly clung to him, her face pressed against his shirt. She may have been skin and bones, but she was still soft and warm in all the right places. And being a red-blooded single man, it was difficult not to let his mind wander. Or his hands for that matter. She smelled so good, he wanted to bury his nose in the softness of her hair and just breathe her in. He wanted to fist the silky soft locks, pull her head back and taste her lips.

She hung on tighter and he realized that she was trembling. He tried to see her face but she kept it tucked firmly in the crook of his neck. "Hey, are you okay?"

She nodded, but he could feel her tears soaking through his shirt.

"Then why are you crying?"

She held him even harder. "The past few months have been s-so hard. I was nervous and s-scared all the time. It feels as if the weight of the world has been lifted from my shoulders. I feel like I can breathe again. Like there's hope for me and the boys. I don't know how I'll ever repay you—"

"You don't owe me anything."

"Yes, I do."

Well, if she really thought so…

"Stay here with me. You and the boys," he said, the words leaping out before he could think better of it. She went still and silent, and he winced, wondering if he could have picked a worse time to spring this on her. What the hell was wrong with him? In the business world he was a shark, but this sweet, nurturing woman had him chasing his own tail.

Her words muffled a little by his shirt, she finally said, "You really want us to stay here? With you?"

"Just until you get back on your feet."

She abruptly let go of him and stepped back, sniffling and wiping the tears from her cheeks. "I can get by on my own. I have for a very long time."

Stubborn to a fault.

"I don't doubt that for a second," he said, then he pulled out the big guns. "But don't the boys deserve better than just *getting by*?"

<u>Six</u>

*O*uch.

Talk about hitting below the belt. Holly couldn't deny that Jason was right: her boys did deserve better than just getting by. And frankly, so did she.

"I owe this to Jeremy," Jason said, and the pain and loss that flashed deep in his eyes made her heart ache. How could she tell him no when he looked at her that way, with so much sincerity and hurt? This might be just as good for him as it was for her and the boys. It might bring him closure.

"Okay," she said.

He blinked, as if he wasn't sure he heard her correctly, "Okay?"

"I'm proud, but I'm not stupid. Even without all that debt hanging over my head, getting by in the city is going to be next to impossible. I have nothing tying me to New York and living in the country, in a small town, has always been a dream of mine. And here the boys will have family."

"And so will I."

Something in his tone pinched her heart. Until just now it hadn't occurred to her that maybe he was lonely, but she could see it in his eyes. Could it be that he needed them just as much as they needed him? Her foster mother used to tell her and her foster siblings when the budget was especially tight that they should not be fooled into believing that money could buy happiness. It looked as if she'd been right.

"I do have a few conditions," Holly told Jason and his left brow spiked. "When it comes to the twins, I decide what's best for them. And this is non-negotiable."

"I just want to help."

"I know, but there's a fine line between helping someone and trying to control them."

His expression said he knew she was right. *"You're* in charge. Got it. What else?"

She sat on the edge of his desk, which was so clean she doubted she would find even a speck of dust. In that way he and Jeremy were nothing alike. Since the day she'd moved in with Jeremy, until the day he died, Holly had always been picking up after him. Shoes and socks on the living room floor. Dirty clothes and wet towels in the bathroom. He left soiled dishes all over the place when an empty dishwasher sat just steps away in the kitchen. She was tidy by nature, so his slovenly ways used to drive her crazy.

She looked up at Jeremy and realized he was watching her expectantly. Conditions, right.

How about no more touching each other? That would be a good one, because pressing herself against all that rock solid male heat had been a really stupid move.

She'd been fine, right up to the second when she realized how good it felt. She was a new mother, but she was also a woman. One who hadn't had any sort of sexual contact with a man since the fifth month of her pregnancy. But if she was going to stay here they needed to have a strict hands-off rule.

But how was she supposed to say that without tipping Jason off to the fact that she *wanted* to put her hands on him? *All over him.*

Eye contact was a tough one, as well, but she couldn't tell him not to look at her. It wasn't his fault that she practically melted when those intense blue eyes locked on hers. And his voice? The low, deep pitch thrummed across her nerves and sent shivers up her spine. But she couldn't tell him not to talk to her.

Oh man, she was in trouble.

"I guess that's it," she told him.

Looking mildly amused, he said, "You drive a hard bargain."

With herself, maybe. But what else was new?

"You're sure there's nothing else?" he asked her.

She nodded, thinking to herself, *Liar.* "If anything unexpected arises—" *Arises? Honey, don't even go there.* "—we can sort it out then."

"Sounds fair enough." Jason held his hand out and said, "So, we have a deal."

So much for her no-touching rule.

She accepted his gesture, watched as his much bigger hand swallowed up hers. And when he didn't let go immediately, she looked up, her eyes snagging on his. She was instantly mesmerized.

Damn it. Another rule down the drain. She really sucked at this.

He held on several seconds longer and then let her

hand slip from his. Slowly, like a caress. Was he doing it on purpose, or did he just naturally radiate this intense sexual energy? Honestly, she wasn't sure which was worse.

She caught her gaze drifting lower and wondered if he and his brother were truly identical...

She blushed at the depraved direction her thoughts had taken, but thankfully her face was already red and splotchy from crying. Which was another thing she never did, especially in front of other people. So what the heck was wrong with her? She certainly wasn't acting like herself. Maybe she didn't know who that person was anymore. Maybe the events of the past year had irrevocably changed her. So what would it take to change back?

Did she even want to?

"Would it be all right if I brought a few things here from my apartment?" she asked him. "The rest can go in storage."

"Holly, this is your home now. You can bring anything you'd like. I *want* you to feel comfortable here."

Weirdly enough, she sort of did already, as if she was meant to be here. Which she knew was ridiculous. Maybe she was just really, really relieved.

"I'll make the arrangements to have your things moved," he said.

"Thank you, but I can handle that myself."

He opened his mouth—she assumed to argue—then caught himself. "Of course. But if it becomes financially prohibitive—"

"You'll be the first one to know," she assured him.

"And if there's anything else you need, anything at all—"

"I *promise* you will be the first one to know."

He chuckled and shook his head. "I'm sorry. You'll have to be patient with me."

"Lucky for you I have loads of patience." She had the feeling she would need it.

"By the way, we're going to—" Jason stopped abruptly, cursed under his breath and then started over. "What I meant to say is that we've been invited to dine with some friends of mine. I wondered if you would like to go. They're excited to meet you and the boys."

"That sounds like fun." She liked the idea of meeting his friends, getting to know more about his life. And she liked the fact that he had asked her instead of issuing an order. "I'd love to go."

If she suspected he was bringing her along just to be nice, his smile told a different story. It said he was genuinely happy that she'd accepted. She wasn't sure why that surprised her, but it did. She just hoped she didn't make a fool of herself. That she didn't say something stupid and embarrass him. Or stare dumbfounded the entire time, lost in his incredibly blue eyes.

The way she was right now.

And even worse, he was looking at her the same way.

What would he do if she reached up and touched his smooth face, if she traced his lips with her finger? Or her tongue…?

"What's going on in here?"

Holly stepped back guiltily, though technically she hadn't done anything wrong, and spun around to see Faye standing in the doorway to Jason's office. Talk about perfect timing. Faye's presence may have just stopped her from doing something monumentally stupid.

The older woman looked back and forth between

Holly and Jason, brow furrowed, and said, "Is every-thing okay? I heard shouting."

Yikes, had Holly really been so loud that Faye had heard her all the way in the kitchen?

"And why is Holly crying?" she demanded, shoot-ing Jason an accusing look.

He held his arms up in defense. "We were just ne-gotiating."

She narrowed her eyes at him. "Negotiating what?"

He leaned close to Holly and said under his breath, "Did I mention that Faye can be a little nosy?"

"I heard that," she said, crossing her skinny arms, and tossing her short graying hair, looking pretty tough for someone so tiny. And Jason's wry grin said he loved to tease her. They interacted more like family than em-ployee and employer. After so many years it probably felt as if they were related.

"I am not nosy," Faye said. "I'm curious. And con-cerned. There is a difference."

"I've asked Holly and the boys to stay here," Jason said. "And she's accepted."

Faye gasped and clapped her hands together, eyes wide. "Oh, that's wonderful!"

Her enthusiasm surprised Holly a little, but she sure did feel welcome, as if she really was home.

"For how long?" Faye asked her.

"That part is still up in the air. Long enough to get back on my feet. But I don't want to be a burden."

Faye waved away the words as if they were a pesky insect. "There is no way that you and those beautiful little angels could ever be a burden. Taking care of people is what I do. And these days Jason doesn't need much care. We need some new life breathed into this old place."

"Still, I'd like you to give me a list of things I can do around the house. Any way I can help out. I want to pull my weight."

"I'll see what I can come up with," Faye said. "Now, come have breakfast, you two, before it's cold."

"We'll be right there," Jason told her, and when she was gone, said to Holly, "I never imagined it would be this easy."

"What?"

"Convincing you to stay. I assumed kneepads and groveling would be involved. Especially after you found out what I did."

She couldn't imagine Jason ever groveling or ever needing to. He was so dynamic and charismatic, and he oozed authority. Obviously *she* had trouble telling him no.

Which had her wondering, as he grinned down at her with that mesmerizing smile, looking sexy as hell without even trying, what the heck she had just gotten herself into.

Seven

"Jason, wake up!"

Jason heard the plea through the fog of sleep, felt a hand shaking him and peeled open his eyes. The room was dark, but he could see Holly's silhouette beside his bed. She was holding one of the twins.

He sat up and switched on the lamp, squinting against the sudden bright light. It was a good thing he'd elected to start wearing pajamas to bed while they were here, or he would have some serious explaining to do. "What time is it?"

"Almost two," Holly said. "I'm so sorry to wake you." She wore an oversize T-shirt that hung to her knees and her ponytail was lopsided. "Marshall is sick."

Jason was instantly awake and on his feet, heart in his throat. "What's wrong?"

The words were barely out when Marshall let loose a throaty cough like Jason had never heard before, and his heart plummeted to the balls of his feet. "Oh, my God. Is he choking? Can he breathe?"

"Relax," she said, sounding calm but concerned. "Contrary to how he sounds, he seems to be breathing okay, but since he's a preemie I don't want to take any chances."

"What's wrong with him?"

"I'm pretty sure it's the croup."

He blinked. "The *what*?"

"The croup. It's a virus that settles in the vocal chords. At least, that's what it said on the internet."

She was trusting the internet at a time like this? What Marshall needed was a doctor. Though Jason had to admit that other than the cough the baby seemed fine, flashing Jason a goofy, toothless smile even as he was hacking. "What can I do?"

"Can you get ahold of Faye? I'm sure she'll know what to do. I would go over to their house, but it's so dark out there I'm afraid I might trip on something or get lost in the woods."

"I'll call her," Jason said, reaching for his cell phone and dialing her number.

Faye answered on the first ring with a sleepy, "It's 2:00 a.m."

"What do you know about the croup?" he asked her. "Holly thinks Marshall has it."

"Does he sound like a collie?"

Marshall started to cough again and Jason held the phone closer to the baby. "He sounds like this."

"Oh, yeah, that's the croup, all right."

"You're sure?"

"Positive. You used to get it when you were a baby."

He told Holly, "She said it's definitely the croup."

Holly exhaled deeply, as if she'd been holding her

breath, and sunk against the bedpost in relief. Maybe she hadn't been as calm inside as she was on the outside. "What does she suggest?" she asked Jason, and he in turn asked Faye.

"What should we do?"

"Take him in the bathroom and turn the shower on as hot as it will go. Then sit in there with him."

Horrified, he asked, "In the hot shower?"

"Oh, for goodness sake, no. In the *bathroom*. The steam from the hot water will help clear the congestion."

That made a lot more sense. "Hot water bad, steam good. Gotcha."

"Keep him in there until the water runs cold or you drop five pounds. Whichever comes first. Then wrap him up in a blanket and take him outside into the cool air. And tell Holly they'll be just fine."

It took him a second to process what Faye had just said. "What do you mean *they*?"

"When one catches something, the other is bound to get it, too."

Again, that made sense. As far back as he could remember it had been that way with Jeremy and him, up until it was just Jason who'd been sick all the time.

"Thanks, Faye. Sorry to wake you."

"Anytime, hon."

He hung up and relayed Faye's instructions to Holly. She stood rocking her son back and forth, patting his back softly. "We'll have to use the bathroom in your room," he told her. "The ceiling in mine is fifteen feet high. It would take an awful lot of steam to fill it."

"Thank you for calling her. I'm sorry I had to wake you."

"It's no problem. Let's go get him steamed."

"I think I've got it from here," she said, clutching Marshall closer. "You can go back to sleep."

He was tempted. He had tossed and turned for an hour or so before finally falling asleep around midnight, but something in her expression said she needed his support. Besides, part of taking responsibility for his nephews might mean a sleepless night here and there, but it was a small price to pay. "I'm already up," he said with a shrug. "It's no problem."

"But—"

"I can keep you company." He put his hand on her shoulder to lead her. There was a slight hesitation before she started walking.

Marshall hacked the entire way there, but seemed no worse for wear. Jason figured that most kids would be crying at this point or at the very least be annoyed. But the baby watched Jason over his mother's shoulder, wearing that goofy, toothless smile. He was a tough little guy.

Jason followed her into the bathroom, shut the door behind them. He turned on the hot water in the shower full blast, leaving the etched glass door of the stall open.

He realized immediately that something wasn't right. But it wasn't Marshall this time. It was Holly who had him worried. Her face had paled several shades, she was breathing way too hard and she was trembling. She was hyperventilating, and looked as if she was probably having a panic attack.

"Are you okay?" he asked, putting a hand on her arm to steady her. She shook her head, and didn't resist when Jason took Marshall from her arms and guided her toward the toilet. He shut the lid and said, "Sit."

Holly sat—collapsed really—and he gently pushed

her head down between her knees. "Take slow, shallow breaths."

"I...can't breathe," she gasped.

"Actually, you're breathing too much. Slow it down." His mother used to get panic attacks near the end of her life, but in her case, she really couldn't breathe. Her heart had lacked the strength to pump a sufficient amount of oxygenated air through her veins, making her winded and weak. A trip from the bed to the bathroom would exhaust her.

The room began to fill with steam. Condensation fogged the mirror and clung to his bare skin. He held Marshall up high, where the moisture in the air was more concentrated, while keeping one eye on Holly. Almost immediately Marshall's hacking began to ease.

"See," Jason told her. "He sounds better already. He's going to be fine."

Holly nodded and continued to breathe slowly, elbows on her knees, head cradled in her palms. When she finally raised her head and looked up at him and Marshall, she was still pale but her breathing had returned to normal.

"Feeling better?" he asked her.

She nodded, looking embarrassed. "I'm sorry. I don't know what just happened."

"You had a panic attack."

"Swell," she said, dropping her head back in her hands with a what-next huff. "I'm stronger than this."

"You've been through a lot," he reminded her as the steam drifted lower and sweat began to dampen his upper lip.

"Thank you," Holly said softly, gazing up at him through the curtain of her lashes, looking so vulnerable and lost that he wanted to take her in his arms and hold her. Tell her that everything would be okay. But he knew that *just* holding her would never be enough. Once he got his arms around her he wouldn't want to let go.

"I was so scared," she said. "If you hadn't been here…"

"You would have managed just fine. You would have called their pediatrician and he would have told you what to do."

"You think so?"

"I know so. You don't give yourself enough credit."

A mixture of steam and sweat trickled down the side of his face, soaking into his T-shirt. Loose strands of pale blond hair stuck to Holly's face in damp ribbons. Damn, she was pretty. He'd always preferred blondes. Natural ones.

"I feel as if I'm flying blind," she said.

"I would imagine that all new moms probably feel that way."

"Yes, but it was so stressful when the twins were born. They spent the majority of their first month in the NICU. I spent every day in the hospital nursery with them."

"What about Jeremy?" Surely he must have been there with her.

"He didn't like hospitals," she said, looking embarrassed by the truth. "Because he spent so much time there as a child. Or so he said."

Had it been Jason's children, he wouldn't have left their side. For a split second he considered telling Holly the real reason Jeremy hated hospitals, but now just didn't seem like the right time. "What kind of father was my brother?" he asked instead, and her hesitation didn't bode well.

"The boys came home with heart and breathing monitors. It was a stressful time. Jeremy had difficulties coping. We were fighting all the time. There were times when he would storm out, and not come home until late at night. A few nights he didn't come home at all. Then he would stroll in the next morning like nothing was wrong. I think in a way he resented the boys for taking up too much of my time. He actually accused me of loving them more than him."

"Did you?"

"Maybe. *Probably.* But I should have realized that something was terribly wrong. I didn't *let* myself see it. I just wanted everything to be okay. I wanted that fairy-tale life he promised me. So I made excuses for him."

"Trust me, we've all done that. Me, my parents, even Faye and George. We all wanted so badly for him to change, and he used that to his advantage."

"He had me fooled," she said, and she looked so sad, as if she thought it was her own failure, but Jason knew better.

The steam began to dissipate as the water cooled. Marshall was awake but limp on Jason's shoulder. Though the baby's coughing had all but ceased, his breathing still sounded raspy.

Jason reached into the shower stall and shut off the water. As the air cleared he could see that Holly was just as soggy as he was, and as a result her shirt clung to her body, accentuating everything underneath. And though she was painfully thin, under the oversize white shirt she was still 100 percent woman. And being a red-blooded man, he couldn't help but look. But only for a second before he forced himself to look away.

"What now?" Holly asked him.

"We take him outside into the cool air." He was about

to hand Marshall over to her, but she still looked a bit unsteady. "How do you feel?"

"A little dizzy, from the steam I think."

In that case it probably would be safer if he carried his nephew downstairs and outside. "Why don't I head out to the back deck while you check on Devon."

She paused, gazed at her son, then nodded and said, "Okay."

He opened the bathroom door, letting in a rush of cool, dry air. "Grab the quilt off your bed and wrap us up in it," he told her.

She tugged the quilt off the bed and draped it over his shoulders. He tucked it tightly around Marshall and himself, so that only his nephew's face was exposed. Jason didn't want him catching a chill and aggravating the virus he already had.

Jason headed downstairs and out the back door into the clear, moonlit night. The thermometer on the back of the house said it was sixty-four degrees, but the air felt cool on his damp face and the deck was slippery with dew. Jason paced in the dark with Marshall cradled in the crook of his arm. His nephew gazed up at him, cooing contentedly. He sure seemed like a happy-go-lucky kid.

The first time Jason had held the boys they'd seemed so small and fragile, but they were far sturdier than he'd imagined and he was starting to get the hang of holding them. What a difference only a few days made.

The back door opened and Holly stepped out.

"How is Devon?" he asked her.

"Sound asleep and breathing fine. But I suppose his catching it is inevitable."

"Faye thought so, too. But this time you'll know what to do."

"And I won't have to wake you."

"But it's okay if you do."

In the pale bluish light he could see her smile, and though it was damned pretty, he caught his gaze drifting lower. Her T-shirt was so damp it clung to the swell of her breasts, and so transparent he could see the pale outline of her peaked nipples. He imagined how good they would feel cupped in his hands, or pressed against his chest. In his mouth...

He lifted his gaze and realized that Holly was watching him watch her. And she wasn't making any effort to cover herself.

"Sorry," he said, keeping his eyes level with hers. "I didn't mean to stare."

She surprised him by shrugging and saying almost the exact thing he had told Faye. "No crime in looking."

No, but looking was like a gateway to touching. Or was she suggesting that she *wanted* him to look?

A gust of wind chilled the air and Holly shivered, wrapping her arms around herself for warmth. Blocking the view that he shouldn't have been enjoying in the first place. "If you're cold you can go back inside," he told her.

She frowned and shook her head. "I don't want to leave Marshall."

"He's fine."

"I don't care," she said, her teeth chattering. "I want to stay. He's my responsibility."

Damn it, she was stubborn. What was he supposed to do? Let her stand there shivering? She was going to wind up making herself sick, too. "You won't be much good to them if you have pneumonia."

She shook her head, refusing to leave. He understood

her need to be there for her children, but she was taking it to the extreme.

"Come here," he said, and held open the blanket, inviting her into the warm cocoon he and her son had created. Holly stepped closer, hesitantly at first, but her need for warmth won out. She let Jason fold the blanket around her and pull her in closer. She stood stiffly, her arms folded, and her skin was so cold it was a bit like cuddling a popsicle.

"You're freezing," he said.

"I—I d-didn't think it was th-this c-cold."

"We really need to warm you up." She didn't resist—though he sort of wished she would have—as he pulled the blanket tighter around them, wrapping his free arm around her narrow shoulders. As his body heat began to warm her, she stopped trembling and relaxed in his arms.

"Better?" he asked.

She nodded, her hair catching in the stubble on his chin, her breath warm against his skin as she tucked her head into the crook of his neck. It felt good. Too damned good.

With the crisis over, the concerned uncle in him took a step back and the part of him that was all man, the part of him that craved her touch, took over. Though he tried to fight it, reminded himself he was holding another man's woman and child, his own brother's wife, his body didn't listen. And if he didn't back away soon it was going to become more than obvious to her.

"This is nice," she said. "It's been a really long time since anyone held me like this."

Another shortcoming on Jeremy's part. If she were Jason's wife, he would have a hell of a time keeping his hands off her. And as far as hugs went, it had been a while for him, too, but that didn't make it right.

It didn't necessarily make it wrong, either.

"Maybe a little *too* nice," she said, flooring him with her honesty. "We can't deny that there's chemistry."

He wouldn't even try. He liked a woman who wasn't afraid to speak her mind. He had grown so tired of the mind games and half-truths. How many times had he dated a woman who swore she had no interest in marriage and kids, only to discover that all the while she'd been picking out china patterns and browsing *Modern Bride* magazine? Though he was sure it was more about the size of his wallet than genuine affection.

But there was such a thing as too much honesty.

"Or maybe it's just me?" she said when he didn't replay. "Maybe I'm misreading the signals."

"It's not just you," he told her, her look of relief making him smile. As if there was any question that he was lusting after her. That or she hadn't the slightest clue how beautiful and sweet she was. Too sweet for someone such as him. How many times would he have to remind himself of that?

As many as it took.

"You're not misreading anything," he said.

She looked up at him, putting her mouth mere inches from his. Was she *trying* to drive him crazy?

"I think we'll agree that anything beyond friendship would be a bad idea," she said, so close he could feel the heat of her breath on his lips.

Jesus. It took everything in him not to kiss her. To keep his libido in check. The only thing giving him the will to resist was the drowsy child lying limp in his arms. He was a much needed buffer. "Are you always this brutally honest?"

"I denied my true feelings with Jeremy and look where it got me. If we have any hope of making this work, if the boys and I are going to live under your roof, we have to be honest with each other. Even if the truth hurts a little."

He could see her point, and her willingness to bare her soul to him said an awful lot about her character. He found himself almost wishing that he had met her before his brother had. But knowing her the way he did now, it was probably better that he hadn't. He could never give her what she truly wanted. What she deserved. Despite Jeremy's betrayal he had given her something real and concrete. Two precious sons. It was more than Jeremy was capable of.

Holly was still watching him, waiting for a response. If she wanted honesty that's what he would give her. "The truth is I really want to kiss you."

Her breath caught and he could swear he felt her pulse quicken, her body go soft.

"Too honest for you?"

"I do, too," she said. "Want to kiss *you*, I mean. Not myself. And no, it's not too honest. We have to be able to talk to each other."

"In that case, do you want to know what else I'd like to do to you?"

She blinked. "Um, well…maybe we don't have to be *that* honest."

"Then this would probably be a good time to go inside." Marshall had fallen back to sleep, and Jason could see a very cold shower in his immediate future.

"I think you're right," she said. He lifted his arm from her shoulders and she backed away from him. "I'd like to carry Marshall to bed."

"Are you okay?"

She nodded. "Fine. Better than fine, actually. It's a relief to get that off my chest."

Her chest was exactly what he was trying not to think about. He handed Marshall over and Holly hugged him close. Jason followed her inside, through the dark house and up the stairs to the twins' room. While she laid Marshall down, he checked on Devon, whose breathing sounded normal as far as Jason could tell.

Holly stood over Marshall's crib stroking his hair.

"We should let him sleep," Jason said.

"I don't want to leave him."

"He sounds fine now." Jason needed to get her out of there and back into her bed, where the light from the hallway didn't make her shirt so transparent. So he could get back to his own bed, before he did something he really shouldn't.

Holly backed hesitantly away from the crib, and Jason put a hand on her shoulder to steer her in the right direction. Though she was all skin and bones, there was a sturdiness about her that was strangely alluring.

"Come on," he said. "I'll tuck you in."

She actually laughed. "Get out. No one has tucked me in for years."

"Well, I've never done it before. If I'm going to be a good uncle I need the practice."

"You make a valid point," she said. She didn't balk at his thinly veiled excuse to insinuate himself into her bedroom, and that was all the invitation he needed.

Her room smelled like flowers and a hint of peppermint, and something inexplicably soft and girly. Like her.

She climbed under the covers, but she didn't lie down. She patted the edge of the mattress instead, inviting him to join her. Though he knew that their being together on a bed in any way, shape or form was a bad idea all around, he sat down anyway.

"Thank you. For your help and your honesty," she said, her appreciation and vulnerability so vivid, so honest, it made his heart skip. She was killing him and she didn't even know it. Turning him into some sentimental fool.

The woman was a total contradiction. Sweet and innocent one minute, enticing and sexy the next. How she managed it was beyond him, but it was screwing with his brain.

"So, how does this tucking thing work?"

"Don't even try to convince me that your mother never tucked you in."

She had, thousands of times. And he knew exactly what to do. But where was the fun in that? What was the point in playing with fire if they didn't get just a little burned? "It was a long time ago, but I'll give it my best shot."

Her smile was a wry one and said that she knew exactly what he was up to. But she wasn't doing or saying a damned thing to stop him, and the power struggle going on in his head, between what he should do—*get the hell out of there*—and what he wanted to do—*crawl under the covers and really tuck her in*—was shorting out his brain. He couldn't recall ever being so enchanted by a woman. By the idea of touching her.

In a word, he was toast.

"First, she would usually read me a book or sing to me," he told her.

"I think we can skip that part."

"Sometimes she would do this." He reached up and touched her hair, stroking back the silky strands that had escaped her ponytail, mesmerized by the desire in her eyes.

"That's nice," she said, humming a soft sigh of pleasure as he brushed her plump lower lip with the pad of his thumb. Her lids hovered at half-mast and her pupils were so dilated they swallowed up all but a narrow band of blue. Her voice was low and husky when she asked him, "Did she kiss you good-night?"

Holy hell, she was killing him. And she didn't have to ask twice. He leaned in and her eyes drifted closed. He intended to brush a kiss against her cheek, the way his mother would have. But she wasn't having any of that. She cupped his face and steered him a little to the left so that he got her lips instead.

It was the sweetest, hottest kiss he'd ever given or received. And when her tongue brushed against his, it was like napalm and fireworks and every other cliché all at once. She tangled her fingers in his hair, her nails scraping his scalp, sending a shockwave of blazing desire down his spine right to his groin. He knew that if he didn't do something to stop this, things were about to get out of hand. But that didn't dissuade him from tugging the elastic band from her ponytail, letting her hair tumble across her shoulders and down her back. He thought she couldn't look any sexier or more desirable, but he was wrong.

Holly's arms went around his neck. When her nails sunk into his back, a groan worked its way up from somewhere deep inside him. She kicked the blanket off and pulled him closer, clawing him through his shirt. One creamy, slender thigh brushed against his leg and the reaction was nuclear. But when she fisted his shirt and tried to pull it over his head, the idea of what she would find underneath instantly cooled his jets.

What the hell was he doing? She would see his scar, then he would have to explain. There was so much she didn't know about him, so many things he needed to tell her. He couldn't help but feel that he was misrepresenting himself somehow. And what if she fell in love with him? Jeremy had done enough damage. Jason couldn't risk hurting her again.

Though it tested the boundaries of his self-control, Jason caught her wrists in his hands, pulled them from around him. "Holly, wait."

She gazed up at him questioningly, sounding a little winded. "What's wrong?"

She looked like pure sex sitting there, her hair messy, her lips swollen and bruised from his kisses. Her shirt had ridden up her slender thighs, revealing the crotch of a pair of transparent pink lace panties. If there was ever a question of whether she was a natural blonde, now he knew.

He cursed under his breath, then cursed again. "We can't do this."

"Did I do something wrong?"

"No, not at all. You did everything right. The problem is with me."

"Could you maybe elaborate a little?"

Not at three in the morning. "It's late. Can we pick this conversation up tomorrow? When we're both a bit more clearheaded."

Looking confused and maybe a little hurt, she nodded and said, "If that's what you want."

"Believe me when I say that it's for the best."

Eight

Holly woke late the next morning, if 8:00 a.m. could be considered late. For the mother of twin infants it was.

The boys weren't in their beds, meaning Faye must have had them with her. She probably figured Holly hadn't gotten much sleep caring for Marshall last night. But her son's illness wasn't the only reason Holly had been awake half the night. She was suffering from a good old-fashioned case of unquenched lust.

She had tried to convince herself that Jason had done her a favor. That sleeping with him would have been immoral somehow, but she just couldn't work up the steam. She wanted him, and he'd seemed to want her, too. Right up until the second he'd shot her down. Though he had looked conflicted, as if the decision had been a difficult one.

She could have insisted they talk about it last night, but something in his eyes told her to back off. Could it have something to do with all the mixed messages she'd been sending him? Telling him one minute that they could only be friends, throwing herself at him the next. Maybe he thought it was too soon after his brother's death. She tried to put herself in his place and imagine how she would feel if she had an identical twin sister and was becoming romantically involved with her widower. Would she always feel as if she had come in second place?

Wanting to get this over with as soon as possible, she took a quick shower, dressed and tugged her wet hair into its usual ponytail, remembering the way Jason's hands had felt tangled in her hair last night, feeling the hot pull of lust all the way to the center of her womb.

Sex with Jeremy had been adequate, but he'd never made her feel this pulse-pounding, panty-drenching arousal. She couldn't recall anyone else who had. Not that she was some sort of sex expert. The list of men she'd slept with was a short one. But she knew what she liked, and she didn't doubt that Jason could give it to her.

She found Faye and the boys in the kitchen. The twins were asleep in their bouncy seats and Faye was loading the dishwasher. She turned and smiled when Holly walked into the room.

"Well, good morning, sleepy head."

She took a peek at Marshall, gently checking his forehead with the back of her wrist. "How has he been?"

"You can barely tell he was sick, and so far Devon hasn't been showing any symptoms."

"Thanks for letting me sleep in," Holly said, even though she hadn't done a whole lot of actual sleeping. And when she had drifted off, she'd been plagued with frustrating dreams. She'd dreamed about the day she found Jeremy, only this time when she found him he was still alive, but unconscious and barely alive. She tried to dial 911, but she couldn't make her hands cooperate. She kept hitting the wrong numbers, or her phone had no reception. And when she finally got through, she and the operator were disconnected before she could ask for help.

Then she was in the backseat of her parents' car, and though physically she was her ten-year-old self, mentally she was an adult with all the experiences she had now had. She knew what was about to happen, but when she tried to get the attention of her parents in the front seat, her vocal cords had frozen and she couldn't make a sound. She tried kicking her mother's seat but it was as if they didn't even know she was back there. She could see the truck coming at them in slow motion. That was always the way she remembered it. She'd read that in the face of an inevitable tragic experience the brain went into overdrive, taking in more information faster, which made the passage of time appear slower. Which she supposed made sense.

In her dreams she never felt pain or heard the sound of metal crumpling like a paper bag until the car was barely recognizable. And while in the dream she knew something bad was going to happen, she didn't feel scared or anxious. She was oddly detached, as if the situation were too surreal for a ten-year-old to process, the concept of death too unfamiliar or distant to imagine. Especially losing both her parents at the same time. And she always woke the instant before the truck hit them head-on.

In real life there had been pain like she'd never imagined possible. At first, when she'd woken in the hospital a week later, she'd had no memory of the accident, but during the following miserable months she'd spent confined to a hospital bed, healing from a plethora of injuries, the memories had slowly begun to resurface. Making her almost wish they hadn't. It had taken more than a year of physical therapy before she could walk without a noticeable limp. And nearly two years of psychotherapy to assuage the guilt of being the only one to survive.

"The boys have been angels, of course," Faye said, dragging Holly back to the present. Where she belonged.

"Have you seen Jason around or is he still asleep?" At the mere sound of his name, spoken from her own lips, her stomach did a backflip with a triple twist. She had nothing to be nervous about, yet she was nonetheless.

"He's out back on the deck reading the paper. Go ahead on out. I'll keep an eye on the twins."

"Are you sure?"

Faye looked at the boys sleeping soundly, then back at Holly. "As you can see, they're quite a handful."

Holly smiled. It did seem that they had been on their best behavior since they'd arrived, or maybe it was the huge financial burden lifted from Holly's shoulders, or the help she'd been receiving from Faye and Jason, that had lifted the pressure. Or a combination of the two.

"I won't be long," she told Faye, then headed out back.

Dressed in running pants and a white T-shirt, his hair wet and a little messy, Jason looked more like a soccer dad than a big shot executive. Straddling the chaise longue, he sipped from a cup of coffee, engrossed in the paper spread out in front of him.

"Good morning," she said.

Looking up, he said, "Good morning."

He wore a smile, but it was guarded and a little uncertain.

Well, no point beating around the bush. "I owe you an apology," she said.

His brows lifted in surprise, as if that was the last thing he'd expected to hear. "No, you don't."

She sat on the chair next to his. It was cool and still damp with dew. "I really do," she told him.

"Because we kissed?"

"No, that part was wonderful. You're a really good kisser."

The instant flash of heat in his eyes could have singed her hair. "So are you."

"I sent you some horribly mixed messages. I tell you that we can only be friends, and not ten minutes later, I practically dragged you into my bed. For all I know you could have a girlfriend."

"I could have a dozen."

She hoped he was joking. Or was he seriously some sort of charmingly rakish sex machine? And why did the possibility only intrigue her further?

"But I don't," he said and she tried not to feel relieved. "I've taken a break from dating. Time to step back and re-evaluate."

"Re-evaluate what?"

He hesitated, then said, "It's complicated."

"I'm smarter than I look."

He rubbed his palms together, as if he was working up to something big. "The thing is. I keep my romantic relationships very superficial."

"So you're only in it for the sex?"

"In a way, I guess. I don't do commitment."

"So you're commitment phobic."

The sun reflecting off the lake made the blue of his

eyes especially piercing. "I suppose you could call it that, but not for the reason you're probably thinking."

He couldn't possibly have any idea what she was thinking. Hell, she didn't even know for sure what she was thinking.

His tone changed, eyes went dark and stormy when he said, "Jeremy told you that he was sick when he was a kid, and that's why no one wanted him?"

"That's what he said." Of course she knew it wasn't true now.

"Jason wasn't sick. I was."

"You?"

"My mom died young of heart disease. A trait she passed on to me."

Holly was almost too stunned to reply. "B-but…you look perfectly healthy. *Better* than healthy. Men don't grow muscles like yours without a fair amount of physical stress."

"I am healthy—" he grabbed the hem of his shirt and pulled it over his head in that purposeful way that men have of undressing, revealing a long scar down the center of his chest "—since I got a new heart."

If he'd claimed to be superhero she couldn't have been more surprised. "You had a heart transplant?"

"Four years ago," he said.

She never would have guessed. And she couldn't help noticing that besides the scar, his body was perfect. Better than perfect and oh, how she wished she could put her hands on him. *All over him.*

"And just in the nick of time," he said. "Another week or two and I wouldn't be standing here today."

"How long were you sick?"

"I was diagnosed just after our twelfth birthday. I always knew there was a chance that Jeremy or I could get it. I just never expected it to hit me so young. As you can imagine, it was a really tough time for Jeremy."

Tough for Jeremy? What about Jason? "And for you. Seeing as how you were the one who was sick."

"It took a while, but eventually I was able to accept the diagnosis and not see it as a death sentence. Jeremy never could. He had already begun experimenting with drugs at that point, but my illness was the catalyst that sent him into a downward spiral."

"Don't tell me you feel responsible."

"Wouldn't you? For a good part of our childhood most of our parents' attention was focused on me."

Maybe at first, until she'd had a chance to approach it logically. Which probably would be tough to do as a sick adolescent. But Jason wasn't a kid any longer. He was a grown man who at some point would have to stop taking responsibility for his brother's shortcomings. "You didn't choose to get heart disease, did you?"

He shot her a look. "No one chooses to get heart disease."

"Exactly. So how can you be at fault for your brother's inability to cope? You could even say that the stress of having the twins pushed him over the edge, but you wouldn't blame the boys, would you?"

"Of course not. As I said, it's complicated."

Actually, it sounded pretty cut-and-dried to her. "If he was already experimenting, have you considered that if you hadn't gotten sick, something else might have set him off? Or perhaps that, tragedy or no tragedy, he would have ended up going down the same path?"

Jason's eyes suggested that he hadn't. "He felt guilty that it was me, and not him who'd inherited the gene."

"I know all about survivor's guilt, believe me."

"The accident with your parents?"

She turned her back to him and lifted her shirt, exposing the scars most people never knew she had. "It was bad."

"What happened?"

She tugged her shirt down and swiveled back to him. "We were hit head-on by a drunk driver. My parents died instantly. I was beat to hell, but I was alive, although barely. I heard the nurses tell my social worker that it was a miracle I survived, but it didn't feel like it at the time. I broke almost every major bone in my body. Including my back. In three places. I was in constant, excruciating pain.

"I was in the hospital for months, and then spent almost a year in a rehab facility learning to walk again. After the pain I endured, labor was practically a cakewalk."

"But you healed. You made a full recovery."

"More or less. I still ache when it rains, or if I let myself get too cold, and having so little body fat left I chill easily."

He'd noticed that last night.

"It also affected my pregnancy."

"In what way?"

"I fractured my hip in the accident so my OB was concerned about my carrying a child. When we found out it was twins, he worried that my bones couldn't handle the pressure of all that extra weight. When I went into early labor in my fifth month he put me on mandatory bed rest. For the next three months I had to rely solely on Jeremy."

"How did that go?" Jason asked, pulling his shirt back on, robbing her of her eye candy.

"It was okay at first. But by the time I had the twins I could tell that his patience was wearing thin. Up until then, in the short time that we were together, I had pretty much taken care of him. I did the cooking and the cleaning and all the shopping. He was a bit like a fish out of water."

"Jeremy could barely take care of himself, much less a wife and two kids."

"Call me old-fashioned, but I wanted to be home with the twins. I didn't mind taking care of him. I've always supported myself, but the jobs I had never gave me much satisfaction. I love being a mom. The thought of passing the boys off to a sitter while I worked nine-to-five had very little appeal."

"I don't think it's old-fashioned," he said. "My mother was a stay-at-home mom. If I had decided to marry, I would want my wife to stay home with the kids. If she wanted to."

"You know, I still don't get why you're relationship phobic."

His look said he thought she was a little left of center. "I'm not exactly husband material."

Huh? He would make some lucky woman an *amazing* husband. Unless he had some hidden horrible trait that scared women off. "You're kind, and generous, and I'm sorry, but have you looked in a mirror lately? Because, *damn*. You break the ceiling on the hottie scale."

He grinned. "Thanks."

"*And* you're a good kisser. Who lives in a *mansion*."

"And can never have children without potentially passing on the gene that caused my condition. A long time ago I made a vow to myself to never have a family."

"But technically you still can, right?"

He shook his head. "I can't. I knew that at some point I might be tempted to have a child despite the risk. That as I got older I might decide out of sentimentality that I want an heir. So I made sure that I could never change my mind. So…" He make a *snip-snip* gesture with his fingers.

She sucked in a quiet breath. "You had a vasectomy?"

"After my transplant. It was the only way to ensure that I would never pass on the disease. It would be cruel to put a child through that because of my own selfish needs."

Wow, talk about taking a radical step. She knew so little about her own family history, but she refused to live her life based on *what-if*s. "That must have been a heartbreaking decision to have to make being so young. I honestly don't know if I could do it."

"My feelings are neither here nor there. I know I did the right thing."

And she could understand why he did it. It was a selfless and responsible decision, but the right one? She wasn't so sure about that.

"Okay, so you can't have children of your own," she said. "There are a lot of women out there who wouldn't care. Not every woman has baby fever."

He sat forward, rested his elbows on his knees. "If you could see into the future when you met Jeremy, and you knew he would die, would you still have married him? Would you have even gotten involved with him?"

Her first instinct was to say yes, of course she would have, but it was a little more complicated than that.

"It's a tough one, isn't it?" Jason said. "I'm essentially a walking time bomb."

"I thought you said you were perfectly healthy."

"I am now. But a week from now?" He shrugged, as if they were talking about the weather or sports, or something equally insignificant. "Who knows? The anti-rejection drugs could stop working and my body would reject the heart. Or it could just give out."

Just the thought tied her stomach into knots. "How long do transplanted hearts usually last?"

"It depends on the person. There's a man in England who has been living with a transplanted heart for over thirty years. Some last only a few years. How can I, in good conscience, knowingly put someone through that kind of loss?"

"But like you said, it could last you thirty years or more."

"Is that a chance you'd be willing to take?"

"My situation is unique. I already buried a husband."

"And that," he said, "is precisely why we can never be more than friends."

As much as she hated to admit it, he was right. The thought of losing a second husband was bad enough. But to lose the twin brother of the first was beyond the scope of her comprehension. Just thinking about the possibility made her stomach clench. No one should have to put two husbands in the ground. But she was so drawn to Jason, so fascinated by everything about him. The thought of never kissing him again, never feeling his hands on her body...

"What if we agree that it's just sex," she said.

He leveled those piercing eyes on her and she felt their intensity to her very soul. "Holly, I think we both know that you and I together would never be *just sex*."

He was right, of course. She would fall head over heels in love with him. "So we'll just be friends," she said, and though it was what he wanted, she saw conflict in his eyes, and even worse, disappointment. It wasn't fair that she should find a man so wonderful, so perfect in every way.

Well, almost every way.

"Are you up to meeting my friends Lewis and Miranda?"

"Sure. That sounds like fun."

"I thought we could have dinner here so they can meet the boys, then go to the yacht club for drinks. Faye already agreed to watch the boys. I'm not sure if you noticed, but she loves having the three of you here."

"I noticed. But there might be a slight problem."

"What problem?"

To her, yacht club meant fancy. And she didn't do fancy these days. "I have a closetful of clothes that are two sizes too big. These jeans are about the only thing I have that fits. And even if I'd had the money to buy a new wardrobe, I haven't had the time since the boys were born. So I literally have nothing to wear."

"That," Jason said with a grin, "is a problem I can fix."

Nine

When the doorbell rang that evening, Holly, who was still in her room getting ready, got a sudden and severe case of the jitters. What if Jason's friends didn't like her? What if she used the wrong fork or slurped her soup and embarrassed Jason? She hadn't exactly grown up on the wrong side of the tracks, but she was no socialite.

Although she sort of looked like one.

Jason had insisted on buying her clothes that actually fit, and after a halfhearted protest, and his insisting that she let him do something nice for her—as if he hadn't done a whole mess of nice things already—she agreed to let him take her shopping for a dress.

He kept fixing her problems, and it always seemed to require that he pull out his wallet. But she had to admit that the sundress she chose for tonight looked pretty darned good on her. With a full skirt and halter bodice, it had a distinct retro feel and made her look a little less like a skeleton. She even took the time to use hot rollers in her hair, so it fell in soft waves down her back. She'd never worn much in the way of makeup, but as a final touch she'd brushed on mascara and applied her favorite peppermint-flavored lip gloss.

The boutique he had taken her to in town had the most beautiful clothes she'd ever seen. All designer labels fit for royalty. And though she knew it must have been ridiculously expensive, after stealthily checking the price on an *eight hundred dollar* purse, she'd stopped looking at the tags altogether. The two sales girls had fallen all over themselves catering to her every request, showering her with compliments. It had been almost like a scene out of the movie *Pretty Woman*. Only she wasn't a prostitute and, no offense to Richard Gere, but Jason was way sexier.

Though they had gone into the boutique with the intention of buying one outfit, he'd talked her into half a dozen, and hadn't even blanched when he'd handed his credit card to the cashier. Holly tried to feel guilty, considering all he'd done for her already, but he just seemed so…*happy*. Giving to others seemed to give him immense pleasure. And she could see where someone with fewer scruples could easily take advantage of that.

She would never come right out and ask him for money or clothes, or if she did, it would be out of sheer desperation. But she figured that if he was offering it wouldn't hurt to indulge him every now and then. And indulge herself.

The knock on her bedroom door drew her away from her reflections, and the butterflies in her stomach went on a violent rampage.

She opened the door to find Jason standing there.

He opened his mouth to speak, but all he managed, as his eyes raked over her, was a mumbled "Oh, my God."

She cringed. "Good or bad?"

"Oh, definitely good. You look…" He shook his head, as if grappling for the right thing to say. "I have no words."

She smiled. She'd rendered him speechless. That was kind of cool. She knew she looked good, but not *that* good. Or was it just that while everyone else saw the plain and ordinary woman who stared back at her in the mirror every morning, Jason saw something special in her. Something unique.

"That dress looked good on you in the store, but with your hair down like that…" He reached over and twisted one silky strand around his finger, then let it slip free. "Just…*damn*."

In a dark shirt and slacks he looked good enough to eat. "You don't look half bad yourself. Are they here?"

He couldn't seem to tear his eyes away. "Is who here?"

She really had thrown him for a loop. "Your friends. I heard the doorbell."

"Oh, right. Yes, they are," he said, still looking a little dazed. "Are you ready?"

"I'm ready, but nervous."

"Don't be. They'll love you."

She would have to take his word for it.

She let him lead her down the stairs, and the butterflies went berserk. But the couple holding her sons and sitting on the sofa in the family room were not at all what she had expected. Jason made the introductions. Lewis was considerably older than his wife, who Holly guessed was only a few years older than she was. Miranda was petite, but a little plump, with jet-black hair she wore long and curly. She was exceptionally pretty, with huge brown eyes, a cute button nose and fire-red pouty lips.

She surprised Holly by pulling her in for a firm hug and saying, in a thick Southern drawl, "Oh, honey, I'm so sorry for your loss."

Holly liked her instantly.

"Your boys are just cute as buttons," she said, bouncing Devon gently on her shapely hip. "I'll bet they're a handful."

"They can be, but Faye has been such an incredible help to me."

"They look just like you," Miranda told Jason, then paused, guilt washing over her face. "I'm sorry, Potter. Was that insensitive of me?"

It took a second for Holly to realize that she was talking to Jason.

"It's okay," Jason answered.

Miranda shrugged helplessly. "You know me. My mouth moves faster than my brain sometimes."

"We were identical," Jason told her. "It only makes sense that they would look like me. And it's all right to talk about him."

Lewis had executive written all over him, from his styled salt-and-pepper hair, to his Italian leather loafers. He had kind eyes, and held Marshall with the ease of a man who'd had children. "How old are they?" he asked Holly.

"Almost four months. Do you two have children?"

"Not yet," Lewis said, glancing over at his wife, who promptly burst into tears.

Stunned and horrified, Holly stood there with her jaw hanging, unsure of what to do. She'd known them less than five minutes and had made the poor woman cry. "I—I'm so sorry. I didn't mean to—"

"Honey, don't you even worry about it," Miranda said with a sniffle, plucking a cotton handkerchief from, of all places, her bra, which was already busting at the seams with her ample bosom. "It's these darned fertility drugs. They make me weepy."

"In vitro," Lewis told Holly.

"One minute I'll be right as rain, and the next inconsolable." Miranda smiled through a sheen of tears and squeezed her husband's hand. "But it will all be worth it when we have our own little angel."

"Pardon the interruption," Faye said from the doorway, sparing Holly the burden of an awkward reply. "Dinner is served."

"Oh, good!" Miranda said, brightening instantly. "I'm starved."

She led the pack out to the deck. A coral sunset served as a backdrop to a mouthwatering meal and lively conversation. Miranda dissolved into tears three more times, but was able to laugh it off afterward. And Holly could tell that Lewis adored her. They talked briefly about their three-year struggle to conceive, but Holly could see that it was a very touchy subject for Miranda. She also kept calling Jason "Potter," which Holly thought was a little strange; she assumed it was a nickname from an inside joke they shared. Maybe Jason liked to garden? Or smoke pot?

After dinner they took the boat across the lake and docked it at the marina. The yacht club was busy, and all heads turned when Jason entered the room. The hostess greeted him by name and led them to a table on the veranda.

They ordered after-dinner drinks and a tray of gourmet bite-size desserts that were to die for, though it was difficult for Holly to eat feeling so self-conscious. No matter which direction she turned her gaze, she would catch someone watching her. At first she thought maybe they were looking at Jason, because he certainly was easy on the eyes and obviously highly respected. But when he and Lewis stepped away from the table briefly to talk to a friend at the bar, the curious looks didn't follow them.

"Why are people staring at me?" she whispered to Miranda, while the men were gone.

"Because you're beautiful, and you're currently shacked up with the hottest catch on the East Coast."

Shacked up? "I'm living with Jason, yes, but there's nothing going on. I mean, he's my brother-in-law. It's totally platonic." Or it was supposed to be. Having feelings for each other didn't mean they should act on them.

"Honey, let's be honest," Miranda said, sipping a glass of club soda and lime. "There is nothing *platonic* in the way Potter looks at you."

There it was again, that strange nickname. "Why do you call him that?"

"Potter?"

Holly nodded and Miranda chuckled. "He's the villain in the movie *It's a Wonderful Life*. You know, Mr. Potter. The richest man in town."

It took a second to connect the dots, and when the picture was clear, the truth hit Holly like a freight train. "Are you saying that *Jason* is the richest man in town?"

"You didn't notice that his house is by far the largest on the lake? I mean, don't get me wrong, the median net worth in town is definitely in the millions. As far as I know Jason is the only billionaire."

Holly blinked, positive that she'd misheard her. "I'm sorry, did you say *bill*ionaire?"

"You didn't know?"

Holly shook her head, and only because she was so dumbfounded her vocal cords had seized right up.

Miranda chuckled. "Honey, you should see your face."

She'd known Jeremy had money, and a lot of it. Hundreds of thousands at least. Maybe even a million. But never in her wildest dreams had she considered that he could be a billionaire.

The enormity of it was almost too much to take in. Her breath backed up in her lungs and her brain immediately started to shut down. Her vision began to go dark, her ears started to buzz and the chair swayed underneath her. Or maybe she was the one swaying.

"Whoa, there," Miranda said, grasping Holly's arm, but the other woman's voice sounded miles away. And she no longer looked amused. "Don't you go fainting on me now."

Jason did seem to have that effect on Holly. She blinked her eyes, willing herself to stay conscious, to get some much needed blood back to her brain. She knew the best way not to pass out was to put her head between her knees, but in the middle of a fancy restaurant?

Would that be any more humiliating than passing out in a fancy restaurant?

Miranda slid a glass of water at Holly and said, "Drink this."

Holly took a sip, then another, leaning against the table for support. Gradually her vision began to clear, the buzzing in her ears faded into the background noise and her chair found its balance.

Miranda was frowning, which made her crimson lips look even more like a bow. "You okay, hon?"

Holly nodded. "I think so. It's just so…huge."

"I take it you don't come from money."

She shook her head. "My parents died when I was ten. I grew up in a foster home."

"I grew up in a trailer park in Georgia, so I can relate. I met my first husband when I was working as a waitress at Hooters and living on a friend's couch. I was only eighteen and he was twenty-seven years older than me with the craggiest mug you've ever seen. But he was sweet as honey and he loved me. He was also rich and I was desperate. The marriage lasted less than a year, but we remained good friends until he passed away."

The sound of Miranda's voice worked like a salve on Holly's frayed nerves. "Lewis is your second husband?"

"Fourth," Miranda said without a hint of shame. "I haven't had the best luck with men, but Lewis, he's a keeper."

Holly had thought the same about Jason, but now she wasn't so sure. "Why didn't he tell me?" she said, and Miranda didn't have to ask whom she meant.

"Jason is a modest man. He doesn't like to flaunt his wealth. He's the least pretentious wealthy person that I've ever met. He appreciates the simple things in life. He just enjoys them in places like Aspen and Cabo San Lucas. He has homes all over the world."

All over the world?

"And he keeps his philanthropy very private."

Of course a man like him would be philanthropic. "I really had no idea."

"He was probably worried you would feel intimidated or uncomfortable. He likes to be treated like a regular guy."

But he was not a regular guy.

"He's a financial genius, you know. A bona fide prodigy. People say that everything he touches turns to gold."

"Did you meet him before or after his transplant?"

"I met him about ten months before. He and Lewis have been friends for years. He was in pretty bad shape back then. He spent most of the last year before the surgery laid up. But that didn't stop him from building his fortune. He worked from his home office and later from his bed. He refused to give up. We were so afraid we'd lose him, then just like that they found a match. But it was hard on him knowing that a sixteen-year-old had to die to save his life. There was a lot of guilt at first." She paused and said, "I'm sorry. Here I am shooting off my big mouth."

"I don't mind." She had learned more about Jason in the past five minutes than she had in the past nine days.

Was that all it had been? In some ways she felt as if she had known him forever, and in other ways she barely knew him at all.

"He was so weak and frail, you would barely recognize him. In fact…" Miranda reached into her purse and pulled out her phone. She scrolled through her photos until she found the one she was looking for, then handed it to Holly. "This was about a month before the surgery."

Holly took the phone and sucked in a quiet breath when she saw the photo. Miranda was right. It hardly looked like Jason, and the idea that he'd been that ill made her feel sick inside. He was thin and gaunt and, sitting next to Lewis in the photo, his skin looked pasty and gray. The only thing that hadn't changed was his eyes. They were full of life. And hope. He had come a long way since then.

She handed the phone back to Miranda, a painful knot in the center of her chest. As his new heart began to wear out, would he look like that again? Would she have to watch him waste away knowing there wasn't a thing she could do about it? And what if her boys had inherited the gene? What if they got sick, too?

Suddenly Holly was the one with tears welling in her eyes.

"Oh, honey." Miranda reached across the table and put her hand over Holly's. "I didn't mean to upset you."

Holly sniffled and dabbed at her eyes with a napkin. "It was just a shock to see him like that."

Miranda gave her hand a squeeze and said quietly, "Does he know that you're in love with him?"

She didn't bother trying to deny it. To Miranda or herself. The past few days, since that amazing kiss, had been absolute torture. She craved his presence, his touch. She loved listening to his voice, hearing him laugh. He was intelligent and funny, and even a little goofy at times when he played with the boys, who also adored him. Even if he had been penniless, he'd be everything she could ever want in a man. "He knows there are strong feelings, but I've never said the words."

"Well, if it makes you feel better, it's fairly obvious the feeling is mutual."

Actually, that made her feel worse.

"If I'm being too nosy I apologize, but I just have to ask…" She leaned in close and lowered her voice. "Have you two…you know…?"

"We kissed, but then we agreed that we should keep our relationship platonic."

Miranda sat back in surprise. "Now why would you go and do that? It's obvious you two are crazy for each other. I could see it when you walked down the stairs together. And all through dinner he couldn't keep his eyes off you."

Holly heard herself using Jason's stock answer. "It's complicated." Which was no answer at all.

"How long has it been since you knocked boots with anyone?"

Holly couldn't help but smile at the euphemism. Far too long. "Seven months, two weeks, four days—" she checked the time on her phone "—six hours and… thirty-two minutes. Give or take a minute or two. Coincidentally, I figured that out last night." While she was lying in bed, aroused and restless, knowing Jason was a floor above her. But he might as well have been a million miles away.

Miranda clucked. "Oh, honey, that's a *long* time."

"I went into premature labor in my fifth month, so I *couldn't* have sex. And after the boys were born, there just wasn't time." Not to mention that Jeremy had shown no interest in her sexually. Half the time he had been too wrapped up in his own contorted emotions to realize she and the twins were even there. And when he had noticed he had been so full of resentment, especially near the end. She hadn't told Jason the whole story. Hadn't admitted how bitter and cruel Jeremy could be. It had been like living with two different people. One who was sweet and compassionate, the other spiteful and mean. Even if he had wanted to have sex, the idea of him touching her had been almost repulsive at times.

She knew now that it was the drugs, but she didn't want to burden Jason with the truth. She wanted him to remember his brother fondly or as fondly as he could under the circumstances.

"If Lewis and I go more than a week I get cranky," Miranda said.

"To be honest, up until recently, I really hadn't given it much thought."

"And now?"

Now it was all she could think about. And her face must have said it all.

"Might that have something to do with the fact that you're stuck living in the same house with a man you're wildly attracted to and who clearly wants to jump your bones."

Yeah, that might explain it. "Like I said, it's complicated."

"Say no more. I know when I'm sticking my nose where it doesn't belong."

The men returned to the table a second later and the conversation turned to a subject a little less scandalous. Holly put on a good face and pretended that everything was normal, when honestly she didn't even know what was normal anymore. And the longer she sat there, the angrier she felt. A lie by omission was still a lie.

When they got back to the house around eleven, Miranda gave her a big goodbye hug, and then joined Lewis to head home in a black SUV that looked just like Jason's. But not before Miranda promised to call and make plans to have lunch in town and go shopping. She knew so few people back in the city it was nice to know that here she would have friends.

Faye was in the family room, stretched out on the sectional watching a rerun of *The X-Files*.

"How were the boys?" Holly asked her.

"Devon was a little fussy, but he finally went to sleep."

Devon had never gotten the croup like his brother. Instead he wound up with a mild case of the sniffles. "Thank you for watching them."

Faye smiled and stood up, stretching her arms way over her head. "You know I don't mind. Did you have a good time?"

Yes and no. "Miranda is really nice."

"Well, I'm off to bed," Faye said. "You know where I am if you need me."

"I should go check on the boys," Holly told Jason after Faye was gone. They needed to talk, but she hadn't figured out exactly what she was going to say. Odds were good that it would be snarky.

"Do you need help?" Jason asked.

She could tell by his expression that he *wanted* to help. But now that she was over being shocked and confused, she was just plain mad. "I'm just going to peek in and then go to bed."

Without waiting for a response she headed up the stairs to the boys' room. They were both sound asleep in their cribs, and though the urge to lift them out and give them a kiss and a snuggle was strong, she really didn't want to wake them.

She backed quietly out of their room, turned and plowed right into Jason, who apparently had followed her up. It was like walking into a steel wall and the momentum knocked her back a step. Jason caught her arms to keep her from falling against the door.

"Sorry," she said, quickly composing herself. "I didn't know you were behind me."

"Is everything okay?"

"Why do you ask?"

"I'm getting a vibe."

"I'm tired. Maybe that's it." She walked to her bedroom and he followed her.

He didn't look as if he believed her. "Can we talk for a minute?"

Probably not such a good idea. "About what?"

"I heard Miranda invite you shopping," he said, following her into her bedroom uninvited. "I know how you feel about taking money from me, but you and the boys are going to need things. I was thinking that it would be a good idea to give you a monthly allowance. Like I did with Jeremy."

What the heck was she going to do with ten thousand dollars a month?

"Okay," she said, and was rewarded with a look of genuine surprise.

"Really?"

"Sure. That would be what? Ten thousand a month? One hundred and twenty thousand a year?"

The bright look began to fade. "In that ballpark, yes."

"Well, why stop there? How does a million sound? Or what the hell, how about a *billon*? You could afford that, right?"

He actually winced.

"So it's true. You are a billionaire?"

Ten

"You're upset," Jason said.

Thanks, Captain Obvious. Ya think? "Can you blame me? You might have mentioned it."

"It didn't seem that relevant."

"Not *relevant*?"

"What I meant was, I was waiting for the right time."

"When? After the twins finish college?"

In a tone that held more patience than she probably deserved, he said, "You said it yourself our situation is unique, and just like you I'm doing my best to figure it out. I'm not perfect. You're going to have to cut me a little slack."

His words sucked the wind right out of her sails, and her head dropped in shame.

He was right. She was being selfish and immature. Maybe he'd been worried that knowing about the money would change things between them. That she would begin to think of him differently. But as he stood in her room, looking just as perplexed and frustrated by this as she was, he was still just Jason. A real man with feelings and not just a number on a bank statement. And she knew, money or no money, that would never change. "I'm sorry," she said. "I'm not being fair. I guess I just thought that there would be no more surprises between us."

He had every right to be angry with her, or at the very least annoyed, but he wasn't. The man had the patience of a saint. And considering all that he had been through, he'd probably earned it. "We'll figure this all out. It'll just take time."

She knew he was right. "It seems so surreal."

"Well, you had better get used to it. If something happens to me, the twins will get it all."

Huh?

No, that couldn't be right. "But…you said Jeremy was disinherited."

"By our father. It's all mine now, and I can do with it what I choose."

"I—I don't know what to say. The idea of being responsible for that much money… I would be lost. Overwhelmed. I wouldn't even know where to begin."

"I would never let that happen. Arrangements have already been made. You'll have all the financial guidance you'll need."

Arrangements had been made, meaning this was not just a possibility. This was her life now. She was the mother of future billionaires. Her life would never be the same. It was so much to take in all at once.

"If it's any consolation, I don't actually have a billion dollars. My money is spread all over the place."

It was a small consolation and good to know that he

was thinking ahead. Not that she would have expected anything less than that.

The last of her energy drained, Holly sat down on the edge of the bed. "Miranda said you're a financial prodigy. And everything you touch turns to gold."

"She was exaggerating."

Holly doubted that.

Jason sat down beside her, already such a familiar presence. She knew the smell of him, the sharp angle of his jaw, the way his hair fell across his forehead. And then there was the electrical current that seemed to arc between them even if they were yards away from each other. The same energy that she was feeling right now.

She wished she could lean against him, bury her face in the crook of his neck and breathe him in, feel the brush of beard stubble against her forehead. The dark shadow on his cheeks and chin made him look sexy and dangerous. A guilty pleasure. She wanted to take his face in her palms and press her lips to his, feel his hands on her skin. She wanted to know the sweet pressure of that delicious body settling over her, his weight pressing her to the mattress, thrusting between her thighs. She wanted it so badly it hurt. And it wasn't fair that she couldn't have him. It was as if the universe was playing some cruel joke on her. The universe had robbed her of her parents, her security. Had given her two beautiful children who would never know their father. It handed her this wonderful man, and then set him behind an indestructible wall of glass. There was no way over or around it. She was cursed to spend the rest of her life watching him from the other side, so close but just out of reach.

"Are we okay now?" he asked her.

"Yes, we're okay. I'm sorry I overreacted. And I want you to know how much I appreciate all that you've done for me."

He rose from the bed and she did, too. "Is there anything I do can for you? Anything you need?"

All she really needed was him, but she shook her head. "About the allowance, you do what you think is right. Whatever you decide, I'll be good with it."

"Well, then, I should let you get to bed."

Only if you come with me, she wanted to say, but of course she didn't.

Jason reached over and cradled her face in his big hands, pressed a kiss to her forehead, his lips lingering as if he didn't want it to end. If he were to kiss her mouth right now she wouldn't try to stop him. Thankfully neither of them seemed willing to take that first step. But the ache that settled in her chest, the deep longing to be close to him could only mean one thing. Miranda was right, Holly loved him. Not just that, but she was *in love* with him. Totally and completely. It had just happened, and now she had to figure out a way to make it un-happen.

The words *I love you* balanced on the tip of her tongue, but she had neither the right nor the courage to let them slip past her lips.

It wasn't meant to be.

A week later, Jason lay in bed in his penthouse apartment in New York, flipping through the channels on his ridiculously huge television, bored out of his skull and wishing he were back home with Holly and the boys. He used to enjoy these occasional business trips to the city, but until recently, he really hadn't had anything to come home to. She and the twins were so deeply ingrained in his life now. He could hardly remember what it was like when they weren't there.

He would have brought them along, but not only had he been in meetings from 8:00 a.m. to 9:00 p.m. that night, he was supposed to be keeping his distance from Holly. Not that it had been doing any good. After that night out with Lewis and Miranda, something had changed between him and Holly. He couldn't quite put his finger on what it was, but things were different. More intense, maybe. All he knew was that it was getting more and more difficult to keep his distance. He'd been thinking things, impossible things, such as what would happen if they stopped fighting it and let their relationship take its natural course. But he already knew the answer. As much as he wanted her, he couldn't do it to Holly and the boys. It wouldn't be fair when his life expectancy was so uncertain. He'd seen the look on her face when she'd talked about already burying one husband. It would be cruel to put her through that again.

His phone rang and he scooped it up from the bed beside him, hoping that it was Holly. Since he'd left yesterday morning they had spoken on the phone and texted numerous times. He'd come to see her not just as a woman he could fall in love with, but a good friend. She saw him for who he was, and he actually liked that she was unimpressed by his money. Intimidated even. He had a feeling that if he lost every penny she genuinely wouldn't care. Most of his life had been about his career and making more money. But now that he had someone to share that money with, and his brother's sons to carry on the family name, making a mark for himself seemed a little less crucial.

He was disappointed to see that it was Lewis calling

him, probably to ask how the meetings went. Normally
he would have been there with Jason, but he'd had some
sort of appointment with Miranda that he couldn't miss.
According to Holly, she and Miranda had been spending a lot of time together. Miranda had been slowly
introducing Holly to the local population and helping
her deal with people's perceptions, or misperceptions,
of what she and Jason did behind closed doors. For
him, privacy and anonymity were precious commodi-
ties in short supply. But he was used to the gossip and
speculation.

Though he wasn't much in the mood for talking, he
answered the phone. After the obligatory hellos, Lewis
asked Jason how business was going in New York.

"I was hoping I could get out of here in a day or
two, but it's not looking that way. Probably Friday at
the soonest."

"You don't sound too thrilled about that."

No, he wasn't. "Don't I?"

"You love a challenging business deal. The riskier
the better."

He used to.

When he met his friend's observation with silence,
Lewis said, "Why don't you just tell her how you feel?"

"My feelings are irrelevant."

"You say that a lot, but I don't know if you really
believe it anymore."

Whether he believed it, or even liked it, wasn't the
point.

"You've worked hard all of your life," Lewis said.
"Why not take a little time off, give yourself a break?
Spend some quality time with Holly and the boys."

Spending more time with Holly was the last thing
he should be doing. She and the boys were settled and

safe, and that was all that mattered. Well, all that should have mattered.

"Will you be driving down tomorrow?" he asked Lewis.

"I'm sending Preston in my place."

"Is something wrong?"

"No, but Miranda has an appointment with a specialist."

"What kind of specialist?"

"An obstetrician who specializes in high-risk pregnancy."

Jason blinked. "Pregnancy?"

"Oh, did I forget to mention that we're pregnant?"

"I think so!" Jason said with a laugh. "Congratulations. I guess third time was the charm."

"I guess so."

Jason couldn't have been happier for his friend, and was maybe just a little envious. "Miranda must be thrilled."

"She's busting at the seams to tell everyone, but we're going to wait a few months to make the official announcement. You know, just in case."

"How do you feel?"

"Cautiously optimistic."

Jason could understand Lewis's apprehension, given how hard it had been for them to conceive. "Does Holly know?"

"Miranda is on the phone with her as we speak."

Jason's call-waiting buzzed, and it was Holly. "Speak of the devil. She's calling me right now."

"I'll let you go."

"Give me a call tomorrow and let me know how the appointment goes."

They said goodbye, and Jason answered Holly's call. "Hello."

"Did you hear the good news?" she asked excitedly.

"I just got off the phone with Lewis."

"Miranda is so excited. She's wanted this so badly. She's already picking out baby furniture and paint swatches. I want to throw her a baby shower. She's due in early spring."

"Do you want more children?" he asked, the question coming out of nowhere. What the hell would he ask her that for?

She didn't seem to find the question unusual at all. "I'm not against the idea of having another child, but I had such a difficult pregnancy. I guess it would depend on the circumstances."

"But if you knew you absolutely couldn't?"

"I would be fine with that. But I have the boys. It's different for Miranda." There was a slight pause, and then she said, "Why do you ask?"

Good question. "Just curious."

She bought his flimsy explanation, or maybe she was just being polite. Maybe she could see right through him.

"The boys miss you," she said.

"I miss them."

"And I miss you, too."

He closed his eyes and sighed. Damn, why did she have to say things like that? He didn't return the sentiment. But considering the time he'd spent calling and texting her, it was probably obvious. He just couldn't seem to help himself. He could go only so long without hearing her voice.

"I thought that I might take flowers to Jeremy's grave," he said, though to him it was hard to picture his brother lying in the ground. It was just a gesture of respect, because for all Jeremy's faults, Jason loved his brother. And he knew Jeremy was in a better place. A place where he would no longer be tortured by his addictions. Where he would find peace. Call it heaven or the afterlife or maybe even another dimension. Whatever and wherever it was, Jason believed he would see his brother again someday.

"That would be nice," she said. "I haven't been back since the funeral."

"Maybe next month on his birthday we could go together, the four of us." Like a family, but not quite.

"I'd like that. When do you think you'll come home?"

Home. That word had taken on a whole new meaning lately. "Probably not until Friday. Sooner if I can manage it, but I can't make any promises."

"It's supposed to be a beautiful weekend. Maybe we can do something fun with the boys."

"Figure out what you'd like to do and we'll do it." He didn't really care what she chose as long as he was with her and the boys.

"Hey, I forgot to tell you that Devon rolled over today."

"Get out, really?"

"Yep, back to stomach."

"They're getting so big, I can practically see them growing."

"Uh-oh, one of the boys is crying."

"Kind of early for their feeding," he said.

"Yeah, maybe I can get him back to sleep. I have to let you go."

"Okay, I'll see you Friday."

"I look forward to it," she said.

"Oh, and Holly?"

"Yeah?"

"I miss you, too."

Eleven

Holly lay draped on a chaise longue on the back deck, trying to get some sun without burning herself to a crisp. The air was still cool but the sun warmed her pale skin. Her bathing suit hung on her like loose skin, but she had gained about five pounds since she got here. Regardless, she would probably have to buy a new one.

Before he'd left for the city, Jason had given her all the information for her new account, along with a debit card. When she'd logged in and checked the balance online, there already had been ten thousand dollars in the account. But so far she hadn't spent a penny. Pretty much all she had done since Jason left was eat, sleep and lie around and play with the boys. She kept asking Faye for that chore list, but her answer was always, "I'm working on it."

Faye probably didn't have time to write it up, considering the way she had been waiting on Holly and the twins hand and foot. Holly was convinced that Faye was clairvoyant, because she always seemed to know what Holly wanted before Holly even knew she wanted it. She also had the twins' schedule down to the minute, and was always there to help with feedings and diaper changes. And even dispense parental advice. The twins were napping now, and Holly had asked Faye to call her when they woke. But knowing Faye, she would feed them then play with them for an extra hour first.

It went against Holly's very being to let someone take care of her like that, but Faye had a way of making it feel okay. She had been giving Holly the time and space she needed to regenerate, to be a productive human being again, and Holly had no way to express her gratitude.

The alarm on her phone went off, telling her it was time to turn on to her stomach. She flipped over on the soft cushion, the loose nylon of her suit riding up her butt cheeks. It didn't matter really. She could be out there stark naked and no one but Faye would see her. The nearest neighbor was almost a quarter mile down the shore in either direction. Jason had told her his property was the largest on the lake, although at one time, before the Great Depression, his family owned pretty much all of the land on this side of the lake.

George was in town getting supplies, which he transported in Jason's boat, so she would hear him coming and have plenty of time to cover up. Jason wasn't due back until tomorrow night.

On the Sunday before Jason left for the city, he'd driven her and the boys into town for a late lunch at the country club, where everyone knew his name. Then they'd walked the busy streets window-shopping. Everyone seemed to know him, and they fawned over the twins. A few of the younger, seasonal employees in the shops even had offered to babysit. Holly would go so far as to say that they'd been treated a bit like royalty.

In the few weeks she'd spent with Jason, the sexual attraction that she had hoped would fade had only grown more intense, and obvious. He wasn't helping matters in the least. He seemed to take every opportunity he could find to touch her. Be it their fingers brushing as they did a baby exchange, or his muscular thigh touching hers when they sat close—which they shouldn't have been doing in the first place.

Before he left for the city, he'd given her what she'd thought would be a platonic hug, but then as she was backing away he'd brushed his lips across her cheek, so lightly it was barely more than a tickle. But it was a tickle that she'd felt everywhere, and his eyes had said he wanted to do a lot more than kiss her.

That made two of them.

That still didn't change the fact that they couldn't, or at least shouldn't, get involved physically. Logically she understood the repercussions. But logic had nothing to do with this. She was running on pure emotion. So it was almost a relief when he'd left for Manhattan on Sunday night.

For about five minutes.

The dust from the tires of the limo that picked him up had barely settled before she'd begun to miss him.

"The view out here is especially pleasing today."

At the sound of Jason's voice just feet from where she lay—with her butt cheeks still hanging out—Holly's heart kicked into third gear. But when she opened her eyes and looked up at him, she was embarrassed to find him staring at her bare bony ass.

To try to cover herself now would not only be pointless, it also would make it look as if she had something to hide. She'd owned bikinis that showed off a whole lot more than he was seeing right now. So instead of freaking out, she pushed herself up on her elbows and greeted him with a smile, doing what was probably the worst thing she could under the circumstances. She looked him up and down and said, "The view from here isn't so shabby, either."

She was rewarded with a sizzling smile. He looked so distinguished in his dark blue pinstripe suit and paisley tie. "You're early. I thought you wouldn't be back until tomorrow."

Still eyeing her behind he said, "It looks to me as if I got here at just the right time."

The deep thrum of his voice burned her skin more than a dozen suns could. He really needed to stop saying things like that. It was too tempting. She'd forgotten how much fun it could be to flirt. What it was like to feel sexy and lusted after. But that didn't make it okay.

Wearing what she had come to think of as his devilish smile, he took off his jacket, draped it on the back of the chair next to hers and sat down. "Anything exciting happen while I was gone?"

"Not since we talked this morning," she said. They'd shared many calls since he'd left. Most of them had been at night, and some had lasted for an hour or more. She'd learned an awful lot about him during those calls, and now he knew just about all there was to know about her. They never seemed to run out of things to talk about. She no longer looked at him as Jeremy's other half. Jason was truly in a class by himself. His quirky sense of humor kept her laughing, and his smile made her heart beat faster. His big sturdy hands made her long to be touched.

"Anything exciting happen in the city?" she asked.

"Nah, just boring business stuff." He nodded toward her lower half and she braced for a butt comment. "You're getting a little pink."

"Pink?" She wasn't even blushing.

"Your back. You're getting a sunburn."

Oh. "My fair skin is a curse."

"You need more sunblock." He picked up the bottle of sunblock spray that she had set on the ground by her chair. "Would you like me to do it?"

"Sure."

The cool spray felt good on the hot skin of her back and legs.

"I miss the days when people had to rub the suntan lotion on," he said with a sigh.

The thought of his hands sliding over her skin made her lady parts tingle. "Well, technically you still can. Sometimes the spray misses places, and it's better to rub it around and make it even so you don't get random burn spots."

"What are you trying to say?" he asked her.

Good question. What *was* she trying to say? She hadn't meant to imply that she wanted him to rub lotion on her. Or had she?

"I'm merely stating a fact."

One brow rose and he grinned that wicked smile, going in one instant from conservative entrepreneur to devilishly handsome rake.

How did he do that?

Jeremy, she hated to admit, had seemed almost two dimensional in comparison. She could sort of understand why, since he'd had so many secrets to juggle. It must have been complicated trying to keep the lies straight in his own head, especially being under the influence of narcotics. The truth just seemed so much easier. At least she had always thought so.

"So you're definitely not asking me to rub lotion on your back?" Jason asked her.

Okay, so maybe there were times when the real truth was better left unsaid. So she told him what she considered a little white lie. "Definitely not."

"Because I can."

And oh, did she want him to. All the more reason to say no.

"I promise I'll keep it completely platonic," he said.

Nothing about having his hands on her could ever be *platonic*.

"Actually," he said with a frown, "you're awfully red. How long have you been sunning your back?"

"I've been out here around an hour, and every fifteen minutes I flip over. Kind of like a hamburger."

"Well, I think you're done. Maybe a little overdone."

He was probably right.

She pushed herself up in the chair and swung her legs over the side so she was facing him, holding up her saggy suit so she didn't give him another peek at her wares. "I should probably go in and take a cool shower."

"If you need someone to platonically rub aloe on your back…"

She laughed. "You're my guy. I know."

He grinned. "How about we leave the twins with Faye and have dinner out tonight? We could invite Lewis and Miranda. Make it a celebration."

"That sounds like fun." She rose from the chair, slipped her feet into her flip-flops. "Let me check and see if that's okay with Faye."

"You know it will be."

"But it would be rude and presumptuous not to ask."

"That's why I pay them handsomely, so I don't have to ask."

"They work for you, not me. I prefer to ask." And even if they had worked for her, she never would have felt comfortable ordering them to do anything. Although at some point she might have to learn how.

On her way up to the shower she stopped to talk to Faye, who was sitting on the sofa feeding the boys their bottles. Of course she was more than happy to watch them tonight, and while Holly showered. They chatted for a few more minutes, and then Holly went up to take her shower.

She took a long, cool one, soaping herself up to get the sunblock off, wishing it was Jason's hands sliding all over her. But she resisted the urge to slide her hand between her legs for some much needed relief. Maybe tonight after she went to bed.

She stepped out onto the mat, and had just wrapped a towel around herself when she heard a knock on her bedroom door. Figuring it was Faye with the twins she didn't hesitate to pull it open. But it was Jason.

The man did have impeccable timing.

His eyes raked over her. "I came to tell you that Miranda isn't feeling well so they won't be joining us for dinner."

"That's too bad."

"Can I come in?"

"I'm in a towel," she said as if he hadn't noticed.

"That's why I want to come in."

Oh. My. God. "Do you think that's a good idea?"

"No. I think it's an *excellent* idea."

Without waiting for an invitation, Jason stepped into her bedroom and shut the door behind him. He didn't care if it was a bad idea. He didn't care about anything but getting her naked and burying himself deep inside of her.

When he'd seen her lying there, her smooth behind rosy from the sun, it had taken every bit of restraint he had not to throw her over his shoulder and carry her to his bedroom.

"I should go check on the boys."

He took a step closer, and she took one back. "They're with Faye."

"I know, but—"

"That towel is coming off," he said, and her eyes went a little wide. But this time when he took a step closer she didn't move.

A long strand of wet blond hair stuck to her plump lower lip. He reached up and brushed it free, stroking her cheek, and something in her seemed to give. She whimpered softly, leaning into his palm so that he was cupping her cheek.

"I want you so much," she said.

"So take me."

She looked up at him, and he found himself instantly caught up in the soft blue of her eyes, the feel of her smooth, pale cheek against his fingers. Good God, she was beautiful and desirable, and he didn't want to let go, didn't want to stop touching her. Ever. Her wet hair tangled in his fingers as he cupped the nape of her neck, and a soft moan escaped between her parted lips. Lips so full and plump and inviting he had to kiss them. But it was Holly who slipped her arms up around his neck, pulled him down to her as she rose up on her toes. The instant their lips touched he was toast.

He wanted to taste her damp skin, kiss away the droplets of water sliding down the column of her throat.

He wanted to bury his nose in the curve of her shoulder and inhale the sweet scent of her, touch her everywhere.

He broke the kiss, his breath quick and shallow. "What do you want, Holly? I'll do anything."

She took a step back, and he thought for sure that she was going to shoot him down. Instead, with her sleepy eyes locked on his, she grabbed the towel where she'd fastened it above her breasts, tugged it loose and let it fall to the floor. "Touch me."

Holy hell. In his life he had never seen anything so beautiful, had never been so aroused by a woman, so desperate to touch her. As if she had cast a spell over him, and he could be satisfied with no one but her.

And he wasn't leaving this room until he'd made love to her.

He felt an almost animalistic urge to yank her into his arms, to nip her skin with his teeth and drag his nails over her back. To tangle his fingers in her hair.

She stepped back from him, her creamy legs so long and slender, her supple breasts tempting him, begging to be touched and sucked. "Come and get me."

Jason cursed under his breath, eyes raking over her, so hot it was a wonder her skin didn't ignite. She loved the way he looked at her. It made her feel sexy and powerful in a way that she never had before.

He stepped closer, his eyes heavy with lust as he slid his hands down her sides and around her waist, pulling her closer. "Kiss me," he said, and she did. She eased her arms around his neck and rubbed her breasts against the front of his shirt as his mouth ravaged hers. He tasted good, felt incredible pressed against her bare skin, even with his clothes on, but she needed them out of the way. She needed to really feel him. All of him.

She fisted the front of his shirt and gave a good hard yank, surprised how easily the buttons popped free, shooting in every direction.

"You realize that's an eight hundred dollar shirt," he said, though he looked more turned on than angry.

Screw the shirt. He could afford another one.

She tugged it down his arms, her eyes taking in his impressive chest, his small dark nipples, his lean torso. She ran her fingers gently down his scar, leaned in to press a kiss to it. She licked one nipple, then the other, and Jason moaned, thrusting his pelvis against her. Through his slacks she could feel that he was long and thick. The brothers weren't completely identical after all.

She cupped her hand over his zipper, squeezed his erection. He groaned and fisted his hands in her hair, pulling her head back so he could nibble on her neck, run his tongue across the little hollow at the base of her throat.

He seemed happy to take his time, teasing her with his tongue, rolling her nipples between his thumb and forefinger until she could barely stand it. She needed more. Right now. It had been too long and she couldn't wait a minute more. She took one of his hands and guided it between her legs. And he took the hint. He cupped her mound, teasing her with the palm of his hand, then his fingers, parting her slippery folds.

"See how wet you make me?" she said, unfastening his pants and slipping her hand inside. He was long and hard and hot to the touch. She stroked him slowly, squeezing and releasing, sliding her thumb through the bead of moisture at the tip.

"See how wet you make me?" he said with a sleepy smile, catching her clitoris between his fingers, rolling it the same way he had her nipple, making her heart race and her knees go weak. "I've wanted this from the day I met you, when you dropped in a dead faint at my feet. You were so damned beautiful, and I hated my brother for finding you first."

"I'm yours now." She shoved down his pants and he kicked them away. Then he reached down and tugged off his black dress socks. When he was completely naked she took it all in, from his wide shoulders to his lean hips, and the long, thick erection pointing upward and slightly to the left against his stomach. He was perfect. Better than perfect.

He slid a finger inside of her, then another, saying, "You're so tight."

He could thank the C-section for that.

He thrust inside of her and the tips of his fingers bumped her G-spot. A violent shudder rocked through her and her knees nearly buckled.

He lifted his hand to his lips and with a devilish smile tasted his fingers. "Hmm, delicious," he said. "I think I want more."

Not just yet.

"Be patient," she said. She flattened her hands on his chest and pushed him backward toward the bed.

"What's the rush?" he asked as the mattress hit the back of his legs, forcing him to sit.

"No rush at all." She lowered herself to her knees on the rug between his legs. "I plan to take my time."

With her eyes on his face, she ran her tongue around the head of his erection, and then took him into her mouth. She heard him mutter, "Oh, damn," as she took him in deeper. He fisted his hands in her hair, guiding her, thrusting his hips to help her find the right rhythm. He swelled in her mouth and she could feel the hot ˍˎood pulsing under the surface. He was getting close, and if he was like most every other man he wouldn't want to be the one to come first.

He stilled his hips, but she kept going without missing a beat. He groaned her name, gripped her hair tighter, resisting for all of about three seconds. His hips caught the rhythm again, and he thrust deeper until she could feel him hit the back of her throat. She dug her nails into the tops of his thighs, dragged them over his skin, and he lost it. With one last thrust he threw back his head and groaned, his body tensing as he found his release.

"Holy cow," he said, falling onto his back, arms over his head, gasping for breath. "Where the hell did you learn to do that?"

She kissed her way up his stomach, rising up on her feet to grin down at him. "You really want to know?"

"On second thought, I really don't care. Just keep doing it exactly like that."

"My pleasure." She knew a lot of women who weren't into giving blow jobs and she never understood why. It turned her on.

Jason's arms went around her, pulling her against his chest. "That's going to be a tough act to follow," he said. Then he rolled her onto her back, grinned down at her and said, "Okay, my turn."

Twelve

Jason lifted her as if she weighed nothing and flipped her onto the center of the bed, crawling up between her thighs, looking like a wild animal on the prowl, with her as his willing victim.

He nipped her stomach, dipped his tongue in the crevice of her navel. "Your skin tastes so good," he said.

And he could have as much of it as he wanted.

He kissed and licked his way upward until he got to her breasts. He sucked her nipple into his mouth, and then moved to the opposite side and sucked that one, too. She felt the sweet tug of desire, the slippery heat between her thighs and it was almost unbearable. If he kept that up he wouldn't have to bother himself between her thighs. She was already sitting on the edge of the precipice.

Tough act to follow, my ass.

He worked his way back down, saying, "Spread your legs."

She did, and he said, "More." She did as he asked, and he pushed her legs way back until her knees were parallel with her ears and her butt was lifted up off the mattress.

He gazed down, watching his fingers as they teased their way between her puffy lips to seek out her clitoris. "Beautiful."

Then he practically dove in, licking from end to end, making her body shudder and pulse. He sucked her clitoris, holding it gently between his teeth as he flicked with his tongue. She arched up, so hot and aroused that she nearly forgot her own name. It felt so good she wanted it to last, but she could already feel her orgasm creeping up, feel her womb contract and release in a pulse-pounding rhythm. Then the world went blurry as intense pleasure crashed over her like waves in a violent storm.

"You are so hot," he said, positioning himself over her. "Look at me, Holly. I want to see your face when I make love to you."

With slightly unfocused vision she looked up at him, and the second her eyes locked on his, he thrust deep inside of her. She cried out from a startling sensation of pain and pleasure. They were joined in a way that was completely new to her. She felt closer to him than she'd ever been to a man—to her late husband or anyone who had come before him. With her heart and her head and her soul. She'd known all along where this had been going, but it hadn't really hit home until just now.

Jason went still above her and for an instant they stared at each other as if they couldn't believe they were really here. That they were making love.

"I hurt you," he said.

Yes, but it only made her feel more aware, more alive. Feeling the pain was better than not feeling anything at all. It was better than longing for his touch but never feeling it.

"It's been a while," she said breathlessly. "And you're huge."

And damned proud of it, his smile seemed to say, but there was a hint of uncertainty in his eyes, as though he thought he'd gone too far. "I don't want to hurt you."

"Don't stop," she pleaded. She didn't think she could stand it. It had taken so long to get here. She didn't want it to end yet.

"I'm not going to stop. I'll just go slow."

"Don't you dare," she said through clenched teeth. "I want it hard and fast."

His brows rose in surprise. "You want me to pound you."

"Yes," she gasped, digging her nails into his perfectly formed, muscular backside, thrusting her hips to urge him on. "Pound me."

He eased back and she held her breath in anticipation. Then he slowly sank in, so slowly she thought she would go mad. She knew pounding and this was not pounding.

He pulled out again, a look of concentration on his face. She opened her mouth to protest, and he thrust hard and deep inside so all that came out was a strangled cry. Then he thrust again and again. Pounding into her until a different kind of pain, an ache deep in the center of her soul, began to build. She was so close. She wanted to hold back so they could climax together, but her body was having no part of it. It said *right now*. And an orgasm of epic proportions ripped through her. Jason was seconds behind her, roaring as her contracting walls milked him into ecstasy.

* * *

Jason's heart hammered in his chest. Still buried deep inside Holly, he pushed himself up on his elbows and said, "Damn."

"Ditto," she said, struggling to catch her breath.

He'd always known that making love to her would be good. He'd just never imagined it would be *that* good. She was so hot and so tight and his orgasm so intense that for a second he thought he might actually die from the pleasure.

"Now that," she said, "was a pounding."

He laughed and rolled onto his back. "Yes, it was."

He had just slept with his sister-in-law. The woman he'd sworn he wouldn't touch. The mother of his nephews.

He waited for the guilt to set in. The shame and the regret.

It never came. He couldn't even force it.

"I *really* needed that," she said.

"So did I." More than he realized.

She looked over at him, her cheeks rosy and her eyes glassy. "Is this the part where we say we'll never do it again?"

"I don't know about you, but I *want* to do it again."

"Oh, good," she said, sounding relieved. "So do I. Just maybe not right now."

"No," he agreed. "Definitely not right now."

A firm knock on the door had them both bolting up in bed. "Holly, are you in there?"

It was Faye, and she sounded concerned.

"Did you lock the door?" Holly whispered.

Shit. No, he hadn't.

Faye knocked again. "Holly, is everything okay? I heard banging."

"I'm fine," she called to Faye.

"Can I open the door?"

"No!" Jason and Holly called in unison, probably a lot louder than they meant to. He flung the bedspread over them anyway. Just in case.

Their outburst was met with a long tense silence, and he could just imagine what Faye was thinking.

"Ooookay," she finally said, and left it at that. But he would hear about it later. She would ask him what the hell he thought he was doing, and he would have to tell her the truth. He didn't have a freaking clue. For the first time in his life he was functioning on pure emotion, where nothing made much sense. But damn did it feel good.

Looking confused, Holly asked him, "What was banging?"

"I'm guessing the headboard."

She looked over at it, perplexed. "Huh. I didn't even hear it."

"Neither did I." Next time they would have to be a little more mindful of how much noise they made. Or even better, take it up to his bedroom, two floors away from Faye's bat ears. Or there was always the option of waiting until after Faye had gone home for the night.

"She must think I'm a slut," Holly said.

"It doesn't matter what she thinks. We're consenting adults. It's none of her business." Though that didn't mean she wouldn't make it her business.

Holly and Jason went out to dinner as planned, taking his boat across the lake to the marina.

As they walked the two blocks to Lily's, an upscale seafood bistro and brewery, he caught her hand in his and held it. If he cared what other people thought, he didn't let it show.

They dined on grilled lobster and drank micro-brewed beer, and then strolled down the boardwalk, hand in hand, stopping for ice cream before they headed back to the boat. When she caught a chill he took off his jacket and draped it over her shoulders. She couldn't recall the last time she'd had so much fun on a date. It had been so long since she'd been on one. She and Jeremy had gone straight from casually hooking up into marriage.

If she'd known then what she knew now, things would have been very different. ·

They got back to the house around eleven. As soon as Faye left, Holly checked on the twins, grabbed the baby monitor and practically bolted up the stairs to Jason's bedroom. She'd only been up there the one time and she'd been so freaked out by Marshall's cough then that she hadn't taken the time to look around.

It was a ginormous suite that took up the entire top floor, with an absolutely incredible view of the lake and the lights from the bay. The bathroom alone was bigger than some of the apartments she'd lived in, and his bed was the most comfortable she'd ever been in.

They made love, but it was a little sweeter, and a little slower.

When the boys woke for their midnight feeding, she and Jason each gave them a bottle. When they were back in bed, Jason made love to her again, and then she fell asleep wrapped in his arms. She slept so soundly that she didn't even hear the boys wake up the next morning. She woke from a dead sleep to find the twins in bed with them. Jason had changed their diapers and was feeding them their bottles, which they both slurped greedily to satisfy their rapidly growing bodies.

"I'm sorry if I hurt you last night," he said, when the boys were fed and lying between them in the bed.

"Only for a second. It was the first time since I had the boys. The first time in a *long* time."

"Because of your pregnancy?"

"In part," she said.

"And the other part?"

She hesitated.

"Holly?"

"After I got pregnant, Jeremy seemed to sort of…" *Sort of what, Holly?* "Lose interest, I guess."

"Lose interest?"

It was embarrassing to admit that her own husband hadn't wanted to have sex with her. Not that it had ever been red-hot. She could count on two hands how many times they'd had sex, and not once had she ever lost herself the way she had last night. Not once had she felt so in sync with another person.

"I felt pretty sick in my second month, so I didn't want to, and by the time I was feeling better, he didn't want to. He said he was afraid it would hurt the babies. I tried to explain that sex was perfectly safe, but he wouldn't touch me. There was one time when he came home drunk from a party. Then I went into early labor and we couldn't risk it. Honestly, I think he was relieved.

"What about after you had the twins?"

"He was in such a downward spiral at that point. I didn't even try. Then he was gone."

The experience had left her feeling as if she would never have sex again. At least not the kind that required another person participating. Especially not if it meant getting herself trapped into another inopportune situation.

"My brother was an ass," Jason said. "He didn't deserve you."

"I tried so hard to make it work. I really did. But the truth is it was one careless encounter that became a surprise pregnancy, and he only married me to do the right thing. I don't think he ever really loved me."

"Holly, Jeremy never once did the right thing. If he didn't have genuine feelings for you, he would have skipped out the second the test turned up positive."

She shrugged. "Maybe."

"No maybe. I know this for a fact."

She blinked. "Are you saying that it happened before?"

"In high school he got a girl pregnant. She was the love of his life, he used to tell me. Then she told him she was pregnant and he dumped her."

Yes, Jeremy had had his problems, but it was difficult trying to imagine him being that cold and heartless.

"She was devastated. And of course she came running to me, the 'good' twin."

"What did you do?"

"She didn't want to have it, but she was afraid to tell her parents, so I did the only thing I could. I went to my father. He took care of it. At that point, cleaning up Jeremy's messes was a regular thing."

"How old was she?"

"Fifteen. My brother was eighteen. At the time, the age of consent was sixteen. He could have gone to prison. Honestly, it might have done him some good. But every time he got into trouble, someone would bail him out. I know it was the drugs making him act that way, and though he did try to get clean numerous times, he always relapsed."

"I feel that if I had known, I could have done something."

"He wasn't always like that. I mean, he was definitely the type to push the limits. Some of the things we got away with as kids…" Jason laughed and shook his head. "Sometimes at school we would go into the bathroom and exchange clothes so people would think I was him and he was me, and then we would go to each other's classes. We were so identical most people couldn't tell us apart, and the ones who could thought it was hilarious. It's how Jeremy managed to pass physics. That and me doing all of his homework."

"So you were kind of a bad kid, too," she said.

"I'll admit I let him talk me into some crazy things. I took the SATs for him so he wouldn't have to cope with my father's wrath, and he got into a good school, then flunked in the second semester. Looking back, I know I wasn't doing him any favors. But I drew the line at the drugs. Not that he didn't try to talk me into doing them with him. But my health being what it was, I couldn't take the risk. It caused a huge rift between us."

"That was his shortcoming, not yours."

"I know."

Maybe the only reason she'd met Jeremy was so that he could lead her to Jason. She'd never been the kind to believe in fate, but maybe in this one instance it was just meant to be. Lying here in bed with Jason, the twins between them cooing and kicking their little legs, it felt as if they were a family. Did that mean she was finally getting everything she had ever wanted? Or was it just another illusion?

God, she hoped not. She wanted to let herself believe

it was real this time. That finally, after a lot of searching, she had found her destiny. The question was how did Jason feel?

His phone rang and he rolled onto his back to grab it from the bedside table. He checked the display and answered, "Hey, Lewis, what's up?"

Holly could hear the rumble of Lewis's voice through the phone, but not what he was saying. Jason's smile dissolved and he sat up in bed, asking Lewis, "When?"

She could see instantly from the look on Jason's face that something was wrong and her heart stalled in her chest. Common sense told her that it had something to do with Miranda's pregnancy, but she hoped she was wrong.

"What can I do?" he asked Lewis.

There was another pause, then Jason said, "Let me know."

He hung up and Holly said, "What is it? What's wrong?"

"Miranda lost the baby."

Thirteen

"No," Holly said, looking crestfallen. "When?"

"He said she started to spot in the middle of the night, so they went straight to the hospital, but it was already too late."

Holly's bottom lip started to quiver. "She must be devastated."

"I asked if there was anything we could do, but Lewis said they just need a few days alone to grieve."

A big fat tear spilled over her lid and rolled down her cheek. Jason's reached up and brushed it away.

"I can't even imagine what she's going through," Holly said. "They've tried so hard and she wanted this so badly. It's not fair."

"No, it isn't," he agreed. "But maybe it was better that it happened now than three months from now."

"For someone like Miranda, who has been hoping for this practically her whole life, there is no better time.

Should we send flowers so they know we're thinking of them?"

"They know. I think we should respect their privacy. They'll tell us when they're ready to talk about it."

"But I want to *do* something."

"All we can do now is be there for them when they need us."

Having no children of his own or even the ability to have any, it was difficult for Jason to put himself in his friends' place, but he did feel awful for them. He knew how important it was, especially to Miranda.

"I'm going to dress and get the boys ready, just in case," Holly said, picking up one twin in each arm, which actually didn't look as complicated as he would have imagined. "Let me know if you hear anything."

"I will. I promise. And, Holly?"

She turned back to him.

"Last night was…" He couldn't even find the words. "Wow."

He managed to coax a smile from her. "Yeah, it was."

He showered and dressed and headed down to the kitchen for coffee. Faye must have heard them stirring because a steaming hot cup of his favorite decaffeinated dark roast was waiting for him beside the *Wall Street Journal* on the kitchen table.

"Good morning," she said as he walked in the room. She left out her usual, "How did you sleep?"

"What would you like for breakfast?" she asked instead.

"Just coffee for now."

Normally she would have lectured him on the fundamental benefits of a balanced breakfast, but this time she said nothing at all.

"Everything all right?" he asked her.

"Of course."

He told her about Miranda's miscarriage and she clucked sympathetically. "That poor woman."

"Lewis said that she's devastated."

"God works in mysterious ways."

Jason didn't buy into that. No one controlled his destiny but him. "Then God is cruel and unkind."

"Things happen for a reason," she said.

That was the sort of thing people liked to tell themselves so they didn't have to face the fact that life was random, and bad things happened to good people. There were no guarantees.

Instead of taking the paper and coffee into his office the way he normally would have, he sat at the kitchen table. Faye was much more somber than usual. Ordinarily by now she would be talking his ear off about one thing or another.

"Everything okay?" he asked again while she busied herself wiping down granite countertops that were already clean.

"Yes."

She only gave him one-word answers when she was upset about something. "How about we save some time and rather than me trying to drag it out of you, you just come right out and tell me what's up?" Though he had a feeling he already knew.

She draped the dishrag over the edge of the sink, and then turned to him. "Are you going to do right by her?"

Do right by her? "You make it sound like I'm a kid who knocked up his high school girlfriend. That was Jeremy's thing, not mine. Are you forgetting that I'm not even physically capable of knocking someone up?"

Faye flashed him that stern and exasperated look he

knew so well. "I just don't want to see her hurt. Anyone with eyes can see that she's in love with you."

"I think you're mistaking sex for love."

"Or are you mistaking love for sex?"

"She flat out told me that she didn't want to bury another husband. I think that speaks for itself, don't you?"

"Women say all sorts of things when they're protecting their heart."

"Holly is a straight shooter and honest to a fault. I've never known her to hold back when something is on her mind."

Faye shrugged her narrow shoulders. "If you say so."

He sighed. Why did she have to make this so complicated? "Is there a particular reason you think that Holly and I shouldn't be together?"

"On the contrary. I think you two couldn't be more perfect for each other. You've been alone for too long."

"I do date."

"Tell me the name of the last woman you dated," she said.

Was it Marla or Marsha? Martha maybe? It definitely had started with an *M*.

He frowned. All right, she'd made her point.

"I won't be around forever, you know. It breaks my heart to think of you being alone," Faye said.

It was true that she and George had been in his life longer than anyone. Longer than his parents even. The idea of them not being around was hard to fathom. Despite what he'd told Holly, they were more than just employees. Aside from Holly and the twins, they were the only family he had. Would ever have. He would never have a wife or child of his own. But with his nephews and Holly to look after he would never be truly alone. It was possible Faye would outlive him, as well.

"I just want you to be careful," Faye told him.

"You don't have to worry," he assured her. "We both know what we're getting into. Everything will work out."

It was five days before Holly was able to go see Miranda, and only because Lewis asked her to. Assuming the presence of the twins might be upsetting, Holly left the boys home with Jason, who surprised her by offering to sit with them instead of Faye, who had errands to run in town.

"I've never seen her like this," Lewis told Holly when she got there. "All she does is sleep. She refuses to eat and I have to practically force fluids down her throat. She hasn't been out of bed since we got home from the hospital, and alternates between sleeping, crying and staring at the wall. I'm afraid to leave her alone for fear that she might hurt herself. And when I'm not here I have the housekeeper checking on her every fifteen minutes. I don't know what to do for her."

"It's not even been a week. Maybe it will just take time." Miranda was the most positive, upbeat person Holly had ever met. She would snap out of it.

"I thought maybe if you talked to her, woman to woman, she might bounce back. She refuses to talk to me."

"I'll do my best," she told Lewis, but even after how he'd described Miranda's condition, Holly wasn't prepared for what she saw when she stepped into their bedroom. Though it was the middle of the afternoon and the sun was shining, the shades were drawn. The room was dark and smelled stale and sour. Miranda lay under the covers facing the wall.

"Hey there, you awake?" Holly said softly and got no

response. She could tell, as she drew nearer to the bed, that Miranda hadn't bathed in a while. Holly walked to the window to get some fresh air in the room, but as she reached for the blinds, Miranda said in a hollow voice, "Don't."

"Some fresh air would do you good."

"I want to sleep."

"How about a shower?"

"Go away."

"Lewis thought you might like to talk."

"I don't. Just leave."

She was starting to see why Lewis was so worried. But who was she to tell Miranda how to grieve? Hating to leave her friend alone, she walked to the chair across the room and sat down, thinking that her presence might be a comfort. Miranda didn't move or make a sound the entire hour Holly sat there.

She came the next day, and was happy to hear that Miranda had taken a few bites of the food from the tray the housekeeper had brought in, but Holly's welcome wasn't any less chilly this time. But she stayed, just so Miranda knew that she cared. When she arrived the following day, Miranda still hadn't showered and the smell in the room was getting unbearable. After another chilly greeting and several minutes at her post in the chair, Holly could no longer stand it.

She got up, walked over to the window and snapped the shades open.

"Hey," Miranda protested from the bed, her voice sounding stronger.

"If you can't be bothered to shower, I'm going to have to have some fresh air. It stinks to high heaven in here. After another day or two I'm going to have to hose you down with Lysol."

Holly opened the window, letting in an intoxicating rush of clean lake air. When she turned around, her friend was sitting up in bed. It was the first time Holly had actually seen her face since the miscarriage, and it was heartbreaking. Miranda looked a million years old.

"If you don't like the smell, then leave. I don't want you here anyway."

"If you don't like it, get up off your ass and throw me out."

Miranda shot Holly a look that was pure resentment, and then flopped back down and pulled the covers over her head.

It went on like that for a week. Then one day, as Holly was in her usual chair reading, she heard a quiet voice say, "It's my fault."

Holly put her book down and walked over to the bed and sat on the edge of the mattress. "Miranda, it's not your fault."

Miranda sat up, her beautiful long hair greasy and matted into dreadlocks. "The first day or two when we found out, I was so excited, but then I started to get this sinking feeling, like something horrible was going to happen. I couldn't shake it. I was terrified that I would feel that way through my entire pregnancy."

"That doesn't mean it was your fault."

Tears welled in her eyes. "That's not the worst part. After it happened, I was almost relieved."

"Oh, Miranda." Holly hugged her and Miranda actually hugged back. The foul stench of body odor burned Holly's eyes but that didn't stop her. "Considering all that you went through, of course you would be scared. I'm no expert, but I went through a pregnancy wrought with complications. I can barely remember a time when I wasn't at least a little frightened."

"Lewis doesn't understand. He has a kid from a previous relationship, so it just isn't as important to him."

"And he's a man. They don't understand." Holly held Miranda at arm's length. "But you have to snap out of this. Why don't you take a shower and I'll put some clean sheets on the bed for you? I promise you'll feel so much better."

"I really smell that bad?"

"You really do," Holly said, coaxing the hint of a smile from her friend.

When she left that day, Miranda was still in pajamas, but she had showered and eaten lunch, and was sitting up in bed watching a rerun of the new season of *The Real Housewives of New Jersey*, one of her favorite shows. It had taken more than an hour and a whole lot of painful tugging but Holly had managed to get most of the snarls from her hair. On her way out to the car Holly ran into Lewis, who had just gotten home from work. When she told him the progress they'd made he hugged her.

"I don't know what I would have done without you," he said. "I don't know how I'll ever repay you."

"I'm here because I want to be. You don't owe me anything."

When she got home Faye was fixing dinner and Jason was just putting the boys down for their afternoon nap. They were down to two naps a day now, and had been sleeping through the night. Which meant Holly should have been getting a lot more sleep, but lately Jason had been keeping her up late.

Faye never brought up the strange banging she'd heard, and if she'd said anything to Jason he never mentioned it. Either way Jason seemed to have no qualms about being openly affectionate in front of Faye. And though Holly was curious as to what Faye thought about the situation, she never asked.

Once Holly and Jason had tucked the boys into their cribs, they went up to his room for their own "nap." Since their first time together it was as if they couldn't get enough of each other, and she had never felt sexier or more desirable in her life. Unlike the men who had come before him, Jason seemed to know instinctively what she liked, and making sure she was satisfied was his top priority.

She was barely halfway up the stairs to his bedroom and already she was wet with anticipation. She told him about her progress with Miranda and he seemed happy to hear it.

"I'm sorry that I've been spending so much time over there. I feel like I'm neglecting you and the twins."

"It's not a problem," he said, tugging his shirt over his head as they reached the top step.

"I think it's actually good for the twins. The last thing I want is for them to grow up feeling cheated. They need a male presence in their life."

"Happy to do it," he said, unfastening the buttons on her shirt and tugging it down her arms. "Have I mentioned how sexy you are?"

She grinned. "About fifty times a day."

He undid her bra and cupped her breasts in his warm palms, pinching the tips lightly, driving her crazy before they even finished undressing. She laid back on the bed, and Jason crawled up the mattress looking like a prowling wolf as he settled between her thighs. If she had worried their first few times were beginner's luck, she needn't have. Every time she thought it couldn't get better, it did.

Fourteen

Over the next few weeks Holly and Jason fell into a comfortable routine. She spent every night in his room, usually waking to find that he'd brought the boys into bed. He spent most days in his office, and she began to get out more, meeting people and making new friends. She'd even begun to spend some of the money that was piling up in her bank account. Holly still visited Miranda several times a week, but gradually, as the summer wore on, Miranda began to recover. She started to see a therapist, and Holly was finally able to coax her out of the house, even if it was only to hang out on the beach or have lunch in town.

"How are things with you and Jason," Miranda asked her one blazing afternoon in August when they sat in the shade in Miranda's backyard, the boys playing in their playpen. They were both sitting up on their own and starting to scoot. Holly knew it was only a matter of time before they were crawling and pulling them-selves up on furniture.

"Everything is great." She loved him, and she was sure that he loved her, too, although neither seemed to want to be the first to say the words. But she knew it would happen when the time was right. And even though he hadn't come right out and said he loved her, he'd showed it in so many ways. He wasn't just the twins' uncle. On some level, she had come to think of him as their true father. He treated the boys as if they were his children.

The scar on his chest was a daily reminder that he could be living on borrowed time, but the truth was she cared about that less and less.

"Have the two of you talked about the future?"

"Not specifically."

"And you're okay with that?" Miranda asked, sip-ping her sweet iced tea and nibbling on snack mix. She still wasn't eating enough, but at least she'd stopped dropping weight. Losing thirty pounds in the span of a few weeks had left her looking sad and haggard. She'd lost all interest in trying to conceive, saying that she just couldn't go through that again. Although on the bright side, she was no longer living in her pajamas, and Holly had even coaxed her out of the house to go clothes shopping.

Holly shrugged. "What's there to talk about? Every-thing is great. We're both deliriously happy."

"Ignorance is bliss, I guess."

Holly shot her a look. "What's that supposed to mean?"

Miranda sighed, rubbing her temples as if she had a headache. "I'm sorry, I didn't mean to sound so snarky. I'm just worried about you."

"Well, don't be. Jason and I are fine. You need to concentrate on making yourself well."

"Lunch is ready," Miranda's housekeeper called from the patio door, saving Holly from another lecture on her relationship with Jason. Her philosophy was: if it ain't broke, don't fix it.

Holly gathered up the twins and they relocated inside the air-conditioned house. The boys played on the family room rug while she and Miranda ate cucumber sandwiches and sipped sweet tea. Well, she ate and Miranda picked. Unlike her friend, Holly had been ravenously hungry lately. It was probably her nightly dose of exercise in Jason's bed. It was her bed, too, now. She had all but moved into his room. In almost every respect they lived just like a married couple. The only thing missing was the ring.

And maybe the sex wasn't nightly anymore, because sometimes they were just too tired. And he did spend at least one week a month in the city working. He'd invited her to come with him on numerous occasions, but not only did she hate being in the city, she felt wrong leaving Miranda. She wanted to stay close, just in case Miranda had another emotional break.

As if on cue, Miranda said, "You don't have to keep coming here all the time. I'm okay."

"I like coming over," Holly said.

"But you must get bored."

"Not at all," she said, even though it wasn't completely true. "Or are *you* getting sick of *me*?"

"Of course not. I'm just tired of everyone treating me like I'm on the edge of a breakdown. It's like you and Lewis have me on suicide watch. It's okay to leave me alone for a while."

"We're just worried about you."

"I'm *okay*. Yes, I'm sad and I'm angry and I'm hurting, but I've accepted it."

"It's all right to take time to grieve."

Miranda blew out frustrated breath. "I *have* been grieving. It feels like it's all I do. I just want to move on."

"Do you want me to leave?"

Miranda sighed and slouched back into her chair. "No. But I want us to have a real conversation. I want us to talk and laugh like we used to. I don't want you to be afraid you'll say the wrong thing and hurt my feelings. I want to feel happy. Happy for me, happy for you. Happy for *anyone*."

She thought she was helping Miranda, but it sounded as if maybe she had been only exacerbating the problem. "I didn't mean to make you feel bad."

"The truth is I'm a little jealous."

"You are?"

"Well, not just a little. I'm a lot jealous."

"Jealous of what?"

"What you have with Jason. You two are so passionate. So hot for each other. I mean, look at you, you're practically glowing."

"That's just from all the greasy foods I've been eating," she said, patting the slight bump of fat growing under the waist of her shorts. "I really haven't been eating right. I feel so hungry all the time."

"That's what happens when you're happy. I was a size six when I married Lewis."

And she was nearly that small now.

Looking embarrassed—and Miranda wasn't the type to get embarrassed about anything—she told Holly, "Lewis and I used to be that way. Now he won't even touch me. We haven't had sex since before I lost the baby. We haven't even fooled around."

"Maybe he's worried that you aren't ready. Maybe you need to make the first move to get the ball rolling."

"I've tried," she said, looking hurt and confused. She set her plate aside and drew her knees up to her chin. "He always has some reason why we can't. He's tired or he has a headache or he has to get up early. I'm the one who's supposed to be using the I've-got-a-headache excuse. Not him."

"He is older. Maybe he's just slowing down. It's bound to happen."

She shook her head. "No, that's not it. We used to be so close. Now there's just no connection. He's completely shut me out. Half the time when I try to talk to him, he doesn't even hear me."

"Maybe you just need to give it time. He's grieving, too."

"Not really. I mean, I know he was disappointed, but he only agreed to have a baby in the first place because he knew how important it was to me."

"Did he actually tell you that?"

"Not in so many words."

"Then how do you know he feels that way?"

"We agreed that if the last IVF failed we would look into foreign adoption."

"That's a good idea."

"I thought so. I thought it was what he wanted, too. I brought it up last week. I told him I thought that I was ready and that starting the process would give me something positive to look forward to. He said he didn't think it was the right time. And maybe we could think about it next year. *Next year?* I'm thirty-eight years old. He's fifty-two. How long does he think we can wait?"

"Maybe he's just worried about—"

"Stop that!" Miranda shrieked, shocking Holly into silence. She'd heard Miranda raise her voice a time or two, but never like that. "Stop making excuses for him. I'm not imagining this or blowing things out of proportion. Our marriage is falling apart right before my eyes. I don't even know if he loves me anymore." She covered her face with her hands and started to cry.

Holly didn't know what to do. Why *was* she making excuses for Lewis? And by doing so was she suggesting that she thought Miranda wasn't clearheaded enough to recognize her own marriage crumbling?

"I'm so sorry," Holly said, touching Miranda's shoulder. "I didn't mean to be so insensitive. I was just trying to help."

Miranda took a deep breath and composed herself, wiping away her tears with the handkerchief she kept in her bra. Now that she was wearing a bra again.

"I just want things to be normal again," she said. "I want us to be happy. The way we used to be. I want us to be like you and Jason. You're so in love."

Holly was, but was Jason? Though she was pretty good at blocking it out and pretending everything was okay, the harsh reality of her situation was that she didn't really know how Jason felt. And she didn't have the courage to ask him. Maybe she'd been focusing on Miranda so she didn't have to confront her own fears. Maybe she wasn't as happy as she let Miranda think.

"You're frowning," Miranda said. "What's wrong?"

Holly gave her an automatic "Nothing. Everything is great."

"You're lying."

"I am?"

"Yes, and maybe no one has ever told you this, but you're not very good at it."

Miranda was right. As a kid Holly had never been able to get away with anything. It was her darned guilty conscience.

Suddenly feeling close to tears, she asked her friend, "If Jason loves me so much, why doesn't he ever say it?"

"Oh, honey," Miranda said, sounding more like herself than she had in months. "You've got to talk to him about it."

"I'm afraid to. I'm afraid of what he'll say. Or what he won't say. What if he doesn't love me and it's just sex to him?"

"No, it's more than that."

"He did tell me that he would never get married, never have kids. Have I just been assuming that his feelings have changed? That he wants those things as much as I do? And if he does want these things, too, how do I know he isn't going to die on me in six months?" Losing Jeremy had been hard, but losing Jason would destroy her.

"And how does he know you won't die on him? You could get hit by a bus or eaten by a shark."

Holly couldn't help chuckling. It was nice to be the one being cheered up for a change.

"Life is a crapshoot," Miranda said. "You can't go through it afraid. What would you be teaching your boys? To let fear run their lives? That's dumb. And it's incredibly selfish. They deserve better than that."

What Miranda said made too much sense. "What if I tell him I love him and he doesn't love me back?"

"At least you could say you tried. And if it's not Jason, it could be someone else. You can't just give up."

She could if she was scared.

"Say you'd never met Jeremy. You were never married and never had kids. Then you met Jason and he asked you out. Would you go out with him?"

"Yes." There was no doubt in her mind about that. She would have been drawn to him instantly.

"Would you break up with him if you found out he'd had a transplant?"

She could see where Miranda was going with this. It was a question she had asked herself a million times. "But the thing is I *was* married to Jeremy, and he *did* die on me. It's a fact that's never going to change."

"I'm a little confused," Miranda said. "Are you worried that Jason doesn't love you or that he's going to die? Are you saying you do want him or you don't want him?"

"Of course I want him. I love him with all of my heart. When he's in the city I hate it. Even though we text and talk on the phone, I miss him so much. He is the most amazing man I've ever met. But when I think about losing him I can barely stand it."

"So don't think about it."

"That's easy for you to say."

Miranda's brows rose and the look on her face made Holly feel like a big fat jerk. "I'm sorry, I didn't mean that. I don't know what's wrong with me. Why can't I just let myself be happy? Things really are going great. Why can't I just accept things the way they are and enjoy it while it lasts? Whether that's a year or ten years."

"Because as women we need to know where we stand. We need to hear the words. I swear sometimes I wish I was born a man."

"It would make things easier."

Miranda laid a hand on her arm. "Honey, I'm not

going to tell you want to do, it's not my place. But if it were me, I would talk to him. For your own peace of mind. You deserve to get what you want. We both do."

"What if I don't know what I want?"

"Well then maybe it's time you figure it out."

Despite her good intentions, two weeks passed and Holly still hadn't been able to bring herself to confront Jason about their relationship. And it was beginning to wear on her. He gave no sign that he saw their relationship as anything but a permanent one, yet those times when it would have been natural to say I love you, all she ever got was silence. She loved him. She loved him more than she thought it was possible to love another person. Not the way she loved her boys, of course. There was no love, no greater connection than that of a mother and child. She would happily lay down her life for them. They were a part of her, an extension of herself, and that would never change. But that didn't mean her love for Jason was any less intense, any less real. The question was did he share that love? As much as she wanted to know, she was still afraid to ask.

They never talked about the future. Once, in an attempt to introduce the subject, she'd asked him where he saw himself in ten years. He had laughed and said, "Hopefully alive," making a joke out of the question. He liked to keep things light and not bother her with anything regarding his health.

Then she'd found out that he saw his cardiologist on a monthly basis, when he was in the city on business. And until she saw Jason swallow literally a handful of pills one morning, she hadn't even realized he took that much medication. It was a reminder that although he was healthy as a horse now, there might come a time when he wasn't. But as difficult as that would be to accept, she was in this for the long haul. Sick or healthy, she loved him and wanted to be with him.

In early September Jason coaxed her into leaving the boys with Faye for a long weekend and flying with him to his condo in Mexico.

"I want us to have a special weekend together," he'd said. "Just you and me."

Of course her first thought had been that he wanted to get her alone so he could propose. But to spare her heart the possible disappointment, she'd tried to convince herself she was making assumptions. Once the seed of the idea was planted, it began to grow out of control. Then this morning, on the day before they left, he'd told her that when they were in Mexico he had a big surprise for her. What else could it be but a proposal?

She and Miranda went shopping for a few last minute items such as summer clothes that actually fit, and with the summer clearance sales, Holly got them for a steal. She kept telling herself that she needed to get up off her increasingly expanding butt and exercise. And lay off the potato chips. But she couldn't work up the enthusiasm. According to Jason, he liked her body a little fuller, and she was sexy no matter what size. But sexy enough to marry?

"I have some good news," Miranda told her while they were having lunch.

Miranda had finally worked up the courage to confront Lewis about their marriage, and told him to man up or get out. And Lewis had said he wasn't going anywhere. Since then things had been steadily improving, and Miranda was back to being her cheerful, positive self. They had even begun the process for foreign adoption. The last Holly had heard, they had completed the application and were waiting to do a home visit with the agency.

"Did you get an appointment for your home visit?" Holly asked her.

"Not yet, but it's looking as if we might not have to."

"You haven't changed your mind?"

"No, not at all," Miranda said, a huge smile crossing her fire-red bow lips. "And we might be getting a baby a whole lot sooner than we thought."

Holly blinked. "How?"

"One of the partners at Lewis's firm has a granddaughter who is pregnant and looking for a couple to adopt her baby."

"No way!"

"She's eighteen, she graduated high school top of her class and plans to attend college in the fall. Premed at USC. The pregnancy was totally unexpected, of course, and Lewis's partner said she wants to do right by the baby."

"What about the father?"

"Still in high school and definitely not ready to be a dad. His parents are all for the adoption."

"That's wonderful! When will you know for sure?"

"We talked on the phone and they both seem like extremely levelheaded kids. We're meeting the expectant mother and her boyfriend and their parents tomorrow. I've never been so excited or so nervous in my life. If they don't like us—"

"*Miranda*, they are going to *love* you. I can't think of two people more deserving or more qualified to be parents."

"They want an open adoption, meaning we would send them occasional letters and pictures, and they might even meet the baby in the future, which freaks me out a little, but they would leave that up to her to decide."

"Her?"

Miranda smiled, barely able to contain her excitement. "She's having a girl. Four weeks from now I could have a daughter!"

"Oh, my gosh! That is soon."

"But I am so ready. If this does work out and we sign the agreement, I only have a month to get everything I need."

"It sounds like we'll be having that baby shower after all," Holly told her. Which wouldn't give her long to plan, but she would manage.

"I'm afraid to get my hopes up, but I just have a really good feeling about this. We offered to reimburse her for all her medical and living expenses, but she doesn't want money. She just wants to know that her baby will go to people who will love and take care of her."

"In that case it sounds like a perfect match."

"I really hope so."

As they finished their lunch the talk turned to baby matters such as which was the best brand of diapers and what color to paint the baby's room, pink or gender nonspecific.

After lunch they were walking back to Miranda's car when they passed a boutique with bathing suits on sale. "I should really get a new one," Holly told Miranda. The one-piece that had been so loose on her in June was now scandalously small. Not only was her butt expanding, but her breasts were, too, so much so that she'd gone up an entire bra size.

They went into the boutique and the salesgirl, whom Holly had come to know pretty well, helped her find the right sizes. Holly stepped into the changing room and shed her clothes, scowling at her reflection as she pulled on the suit. "I really need to go on a diet."

"Let's see it," Miranda said.

Holly stepped out of the dressing room. "I think it might be too small."

Miranda looked her up and down, and got a weird look on her face. The salesgirl was looking at her a little strangely, too. "Ugh, is it really that bad?"

"Could you go and fetch her a size bigger?" Miranda asked the salesgirl.

"I'll see if we have one," she said, scurrying off, her brows furrowed.

Before Holly could comment, Miranda grabbed her arm and dragged her back into the dressing room. "Is there something you need to tell me?"

Confused, Holly said, "No, why?"

"Is it my imagination or have you gained most of your weight in your stomach area."

Holly sighed. "It's gross, I know."

"Is that how you usually gain weight? In your stomach like that?"

"I'm not sure. I've always been naturally thin. The only other time I gained this much weight is when I was pregnant with the…" She trailed off as the meaning of Miranda's reaction sank in.

"No," Holly said. "I know what you're thinking and it can't be possible."

"Honey, one thing I've learned is that nothing is impossible."

"No, I mean it's really impossible. Jason had a vasectomy. He literally can't get me pregnant."

"It's rare, but vasectomies sometimes fail. My cousin in Louisiana and her husband popped out four rug rats all a year apart and not on purpose. So after baby number four he went in and got snipped. A year later they had baby number five."

"You're kidding," Holly said, but her stomach was starting to sink and her heart had risen up in her throat to somewhere just below her vocal chords. "That didn't really happen."

"I swear on my mother's grave," Miranda said, laying her hand over her heart. "Have you two used protection?"

"No," Holly said. "Why would we bother?"

"What about your periods? Have you missed any?"

She felt a little sick to her stomach. "My periods have always been kind of screwy. Sometimes I'll go a month or two and barely spot."

"How long have you gone without one?"

"Um…" She tried to recall when she'd had her last full period and honestly couldn't. "I don't remember. But I don't feel pregnant. I was sick from my second to fifth month with the boys. I could barely function."

"According to my cousin not every pregnancy is the same."

"But if I were pregnant enough to already be showing, I would have to be past my third month at least."

"My cousin also said that she showed sooner with her later pregnancies. And I've heard that women carrying twins show a lot faster."

Twins? She shook her head. "No, what are the odds that I would have twins again?"

"About the same as they were the first time, considering Jason is a twin."

"It can't be," Holly said. "It just can't."

"When did you and Jason start sleeping together?"

"I don't know. Maybe three months…" She trailed off. No. No way. It wasn't possible.

But what if it is? her inner voice nagged.

"Well, there's only one way to know for sure," Miranda said. "We need a pregnancy test, and we need it right now."

Thinking that this had to be a mistake, that she had more potato chips in her belly than baby, Holly let Miranda walk her to the pharmacy where they picked out a test.

"We should get the two pack," Miranda said.

"Why?"

"Just trust me."

Miranda's fertility struggles were common knowledge in town, so when she dropped the package on the counter the cashier just assumed it was for her.

"Good luck!" the woman said as she dropped it in a bag, giving Miranda a thumbs-up.

Miranda smiled and returned the gesture, mumbling something not so nice under her breath as they were walking out the door, telling Holly, "Sometimes I really hate living in a small town."

Jason was working in his home office today so taking the test there was out of the question. They drove to Miranda's house instead and went straight to the master bath.

"I still think this is a waste of time," Holly said as she had second thoughts about the whole thing. Or did she think that by not knowing for sure there was no way it could be true?

"I'm not letting you back out now. You want me in or out?"

This was all Miranda's idea. There was no way Holly was doing this alone. "Definitely in."

She opened the box and started reading the directions, which Miranda promptly plucked from her hand. "You pee on the stick. It's not complicated."

Holly was so convinced it was impossible that when the word *Pregnant* appeared in the little window after about ten seconds instead of the typical five minutes, she was convinced something was wrong with the test. But when the second test did the same thing, her heart practically turned inside out.

"You're not just pregnant," Miranda said. "You're superpregnant."

"It can't be," Holly said. "They must both be defective."

"Now you're just rationalizing."

It was that or have a full-blown panic attack. "How did this happen?"

"I'm going to assume that's a rhetorical question," Miranda said, a huge goofy smile on her face.

"You're smiling," Holly said in horror. "Don't smile. This is a disaster. What am I going to tell Jason?"

"You could start with *I'm pregnant*, then go from there."

Her legs weak and shaky, Holly leaned against the sink for support. "He got a vasectomy for a reason. He doesn't want kids. Ever."

"Honey, it takes two to tango. Unless you got yourself pregnant, he's just as responsible for this little miracle as you. Or two little miracles if it's twins."

"I never should have taken the test," Holly said.

"Why? So you could be one of those women who has no idea they're pregnant and gives birth on the toilet? I can't imagine anything less dignified. Test or no test, there's no question, honey. You're pregnant."

Fifteen

Holly hung out at Miranda's house for a while, trying to decide what to say, how to approach the topic in a way that wouldn't completely freak out Jason. But around dinnertime Miranda pretty much shoved her out the door. "Stop being such a drama queen and just tell him. It'll be okay, I promise."

Holly didn't believe her, but she went home. She couldn't stay away forever.

When she got there Faye was gone and Jason wasn't in his office. She headed up to their bedroom—yes, *their* bedroom—to look for him. And when she reached the top of the stairs and saw where he was her heart climbed way up into her throat and tears choked her.

Jason was lying in bed dozing with a twin on either side curled up against him, their sweet little heads resting on his chest. Like an adorable Jason sandwich. She found herself wishing that he was their real father or that he at least wanted the job. In her opinion he was born to be a father. It was Jason who could always draw a laugh or a smile from them when they were cranky. It was he who rocked them to sleep when they woke up in the middle of the night fussy and didn't want Mommy. He got up with them nearly every morning when he wasn't traveling, and was almost always there to tuck them in at night. He fed them and changed them. He marveled over each new milestone they reached, beaming with the pride of a real father. In almost every way he *was* their father. Didn't it make sense that he would be happy to learn he would become a father himself? As much as he loved the boys, how couldn't he be?

But what if he isn't? a vicious little voice in her head mocked. *You don't even know if he loves you.*

It was true that he had never said the words, but that didn't mean anything. They were talking about a man who had been hesitant to tell her about his financial status for fear that she would feel intimidated or overwhelmed. Her happiness and well-being obviously meant a lot to him. So much so that she was almost positive the surprise he mentioned today was an engagement ring. He would get down on one knee, maybe in the sand at sunset, and then he would tell her he loved her, and that he wanted to spend the rest of his life with her. Then he would produce the ring and ask her to marry him. However he did it she knew it would be incredibly romantic, because that was just the kind of man he was. He would make sure everything was perfect. And of course she would say yes. She would slip the ring onto her finger—and of course it would be a perfect fit—then throw herself into his arms.

That would be the best time to tell him, she realized. What could be a better conclusion to a romantic proposal? If she told him today, he would probably feel obligated to propose right away, thereby ruining the beautiful event that he had already planned.

Yes, that was definitely the best way to go. She would wait for the proposal and then tell him that she was pregnant. He would be thrilled beyond words, and as soon as they got home he would go with her to the doctor. And if the doctor heard two heartbeats, the way he had with the boys, Jason would be doubly thrilled. She just knew it.

"You're home."

She shook herself out of her daydream and realized Jason was awake and looking up at her.

"I'm home," she agreed.

He looked down at the boys sleeping soundly, sprawled on his chest, and smiled. "They were fussy. I think they're cutting teeth. I guess I nodded off."

"You want me to take them?"

He yawned and shook his head. "That's okay. I like holding them."

In that instant, she loved him even more. Loved him so much it felt as if her heart would burst. She thought back to when Miranda had told her that she couldn't go through life afraid. Maybe her friend was right. It was time to stop living in fear of what could happen and get on with her life. It was time that she let herself have faith in someone. Maybe he was worth the risk.

"Did you get everything you need for the trip?" he asked her.

She sat on the mattress beside them. "Almost everything. I couldn't find a bathing suit that I didn't look horrifying in."

He made a *pft* sound, the way he always did when

she complained about her recent weight gain. Wouldn't he be surprised when she told him the reason behind it.

"You would look sexy in a burlap sack," he said, reaching over to take her hand, drawing it to his lips to kiss it. "I prefer a woman with meat on her bones," he said with a sexy grin, wiggling his eyebrows.

God, he was gorgeous. Though they were identical twins, Jeremy had never looked this good to her. He'd never given her butterflies in her stomach or made her heart race when he'd smiled at her. More and more she had come to believe that she and Jeremy had not been meant to be. That their relationship had been merely the bridge that had brought her to Jason. She was just sorry that Jeremy had had to die to make it happen. And she hoped that from somewhere in the afterlife he was smiling down on them. She hoped he was happy for her. Happy for his children that a man so wonderful had stepped in to take care of them and love them as if they were his own.

"We leave for the airport at 7:00 a.m.," Jason reminded her. "Make sure you're packed and ready."

"Oh, I will be."

"Are you excited?"

Like he would not believe. "A little nervous about the flying part."

"Don't be. It's even safer than traveling in a car, and I know the pilot personally."

She hadn't been at all surprised when he'd told her they would take a private jet to their destination. Jason was a modest man, but he definitely enjoyed the finer things in life.

"I can't wait to get you alone," he said and the heat in his eyes made her shiver.

"And once you have me alone, what will you do with me?"

"Tell you what," he said with a grin. "Let's get these little guys into bed and I'll give you a sneak preview."

Holly lay stretched out in a lounge chair on the resort's private beach, thinking that she could really get used to this. Eating gourmet food, drinking expensive champagne—which she hadn't actually consumed, but instead had dumped in the sand when no one was looking—getting waited on hand and foot and making love until the sun came up.

She glanced over at Jason, who was in the chair beside hers sound asleep. So far they had gone snorkeling and shell hunting. They had visited museums and art galleries. They'd been on an ATV tour, which actually had been a little scary until she'd gotten the hang of it, and wandered through a small village where they'd dined on the local food and danced to a mariachi band until late into the night. And of course there had been sex. Lots and lots of sex.

All of that, and with only one night left, she still didn't have a ring on her finger. But that was Jason. He liked to draw out the suspense. At least, she hoped that was what he was doing. This morning he had asked if she was ready for her surprise and her heart had jumped up into her throat.

Then he'd grinned and told her that she would have to wait a little bit longer, meaning he had to be planning to do it tonight. And then she would be free to tell him the good news. And he would be thrilled, and they would live happily ever after. Though the idea of having twins again had sort of freaked her out at first, the more she thought about it the more she was getting used to the idea. And wouldn't it be perfect if it was identical twin girls? Little sisters the boys could play with, and occasionally pick on of course, because that was what brothers did. But they would love their sisters and they would protect them and beat up anyone who tried to hurt them.

Well, maybe not beat up, but they would be excellent protectors. And though four kids under two years old would be a handful, even with Faye, they could afford a nanny, or even a team of nannies, though she preferred to do the majority of the parenting herself. Whatever the situation, Jason would make sure everyone was taken care of.

"You okay?" Jason asked sleepily from beside her.

"Fine," she said. Better than fine. She was by far the happiest she had been in her whole life.

"You looked like maybe you had a stomach ache."

She looked down and realized she had one hand cupped over the tiny baby bump. It was habit, and something she was sure all pregnant women did, but until she made the announcement later tonight—and it would be later tonight—she would have to be more careful.

"I'm just a little hungry."

"We could go back to the condo and get a bite to eat to hold us over. Or we could do something to distract ourselves until dinner," he said.

"A distraction sounds good." Anything to make the day go faster.

He pushed himself up from the chair and held a hand out to give her a boost. He probably would be doing that a lot in the near future. Especially if she was having twins. Though she had no idea how far along she was yet, she felt really good. Maybe this pregnancy would be easier and she would be spared the disheartening complications of the first time. Maybe being so happy and being with a man she loved, and who loved her back, would make all the difference in the world.

They made love for several hours, and then she must have fallen asleep because when she heard Jason's voice calling to her and she opened her eyes, the room was dark.

She sat up and blinked herself awake. "What time is it?"

"Almost seven."

"I didn't mean to sleep so long."

"That's okay. It gave me time to prepare."

"Prepare what?"

He grinned. "You'll see. Why don't you hop in the shower and get dressed. I'll let you know when it's safe to come downstairs."

"Safe?"

"We're eating in tonight."

So nervous and excited that she could barely contain it, she showered and put on the dress she had bought specifically with this night in mind. She dried her hair and left it loose, the way Jason liked it most, and even put on eyeliner and mascara, which he'd told her he could take or leave because she was beautiful and sexy just the way she was and didn't need any extra help.

She was smoothing on a bit of peppermint lip gloss when Jason returned, dressed in a casual but expensive suit. "Are you ready?"

He had no idea. "Ready as I'll ever be."

He offered his hand and led her down the stairs and out onto the veranda where dozens and dozens of candles flickered in the warm breeze blowing off the ocean.

"Oh, my God," she whispered. "This is amazing."

He gestured to the small round table where they usually had their morning coffee, and it was set for a multi-course gourmet meal. She was so excited and nervous that her hands started shaking and she had no idea how she was going to make it through dinner. Especially one with more than one course.

A waiter from the resort served them, one excruciating course at a time, but she was so nervous she could barely choke down a thing.

"You're not eating much," he said. "You don't like it?"

"It's delicious."

"Maybe you're nervous about your surprise?"

She nodded. "A little."

"We could skip dessert."

Yes, please. "I doubt I would eat much anyway."

After the waiter cleared the table, Jason dismissed him, but not before handing him a hefty tip. Jason always tipped well, even if the service was less than stellar.

When he sat back down Holly was literally on the edge of her seat. Another inch and she probably would fall off the chair.

"Are you ready for your surprise?" he asked and she nodded. She assumed he would want to take a walk on the beach or at least get on one knee, but still sitting at the table he reached into the side pocket of his jacket and she held her breath.

"I know you're not crazy about flashy jewelry," he said with a grin, "and me spending a lot of money on you. But for this I hope you'll make an exception."

In his hand was a small black velvet box, the ideal size to hold a ring. He set it down on the table and slid it across to her, and for a second she just stared. Waiting for him to say something.

"Aren't you going to open it?"

Maybe he wanted her to open it and see it first, then he would get down on his knee to propose. That had to be it.

She reached out and took the box, noting that it felt pretty heavy, which could mean it was a huge rock, though she would have been just as happy if it was a chip.

Heart racing, she slowly lifted the top and on a bed of red satin sat…

She blinked. Then blinked again.

A pair of diamond stud earrings.

Huh?

Mouth hanging open, she looked up at Jason and he smiled, obviously thinking that she was stunned into silence by the beauty of his gift.

"Every woman should have a pair of diamond studs," he said. "They go with everything."

They sure did. And they were exquisitely beautiful, but they were not an engagement ring. Not even close. There had been no proposal, no confessions of true love. Nothing. Just a stupid pair of earrings that probably had cost him a fortune. But that sure didn't mean he loved her.

This entire trip had been a farce. Her happily ever after another figment of her imagination.

"Holly, are you okay?"

She looked up at him and he was no longer smiling.

"If you don't like the earrings—"

"Jason, do you love me?"

He sat back as if he'd been struck. "What?"

"You heard me. *Do. You. Love. Me?*"

He looked baffled, as if he hadn't a clue how to respond or why she was shouting at him.

"It's a simple question," she said so loudly she was sure the people in the neighboring condos could hear her, but she didn't care. She couldn't have helped it if she had. "Do you love me? Yes or no."

"Maybe this is something we should talk about."

"Yes, let's," she said, her voice rising in pitch until she was shrieking. *"Because I'm pregnant!"*

His slack-jawed, bewildered look was more than she could take. The room went fuzzy and her chair began to sway beneath her, and the last thing she heard as she lost consciousness was the thump of her body hitting the floor.

Sixteen

Holly woke from a haze to find Jason kneeling over her, and for a second she thought she was back in her apartment in New York, passed out from seeing Jeremy's ghost, and wondering if it had all just been some strange vivid dream. But as her vision cleared she realized they were still in the condo in Mexico, and it was all very real.

"Are you okay?" Jason asked, and she nodded, even though she was just about the furthest she'd ever been from okay. And she felt embarrassed and stupid and completely heartbroken. How could she have blown this whole thing out of proportion? How could she have been so presumptuous? And she couldn't believe that she hadn't merely informed Jason that she was pregnant, she had screamed it at him. He must have thought she was a loon.

He offered a hand to help her sit up and said, "You know, we really have to stop meeting like this."

In spite of herself she laughed, because the only other option was to cry, and she didn't want to cry. She just wanted to disappear. "I'm sorry I shouted at you."

"You're pregnant?"

"I guess this wasn't the ideal way to break the news." She didn't know if there was an ideal way.

"How? I had a vasectomy."

"That's what I thought, but according to Miranda, they can magically reverse themselves."

He shook his head. "No shit."

She shrugged. "Who knew?"

"Well, thank God for small miracles."

Wait? What? "What does that mean?"

"When I had the procedure done it made sense. Then I met you and fell in love with you, and I began to realize what a huge mistake I'd made."

"You fell in love with me?"

"Pretty much from the minute I met you."

"Then why didn't you say anything?"

"What was I supposed to say? You made it pretty clear that you didn't want to bury another husband. Whether I loved you or not, it didn't seem to make much difference. And to be fair, you never said it, either."

No, she hadn't, but she would say it now. "I love you, Jason. I never knew I could love someone the way I love you."

"Well," he said with a grin, "I'm glad we've got that settled."

"I'm so sorry that I freaked out like that."

"It's okay. And if you really don't like the earrings we can take them back, or exchange them for something else. Like a diamond ring."

She gasped.

"It took you passing out for my dumb ass to figure

out what was happening. The trip and the fancy dinner and the 'surprise' I kept talking about. You thought I was going to propose, didn't you?"

Embarrassed, she nodded.

"Damn," he said, shaking his head. "I am so sorry. If I had known that you wanted me to propose I wouldn't have hesitated. But knowing the way you felt I thought that even earrings would be pushing it. I thought that if I hyped it you wouldn't be able to say no. I guess I went a little overboard."

"You know, it really doesn't matter now. You love me."

"Yes," he said, stroking her hair back from her face. "I do."

"And I love you, too. And I don't care about what might happen in the future. I want to make the best of every minute, whether we have one year or fifty. I want us to be a family."

"I want that, too." He cupped her face in his hand. "You, me, the boys and the baby."

"Out of curiosity, how would you feel if it were two babies?"

"Two?"

"Miranda seems to think that because you're a twin, it's a distinct possibility."

He grinned. "Then we're going to have a *big* family, I guess."

"I've never been one to believe in fate or karma but look at us. I survived an unsurvivable car crash. You got a new heart just in the nick of time, while you were at death's door. You had a vasectomy and still managed to knock me up."

"A failed vasectomy," he said, shaking his head

and laughing. "The possibility never even crossed my mind."

"Is it just me or do you get the feeling the universe is trying to tell us something?"

"Well, if the universe thinks we should be together," he said, cradling her face in his hands, pressing the sweetest kiss against her lips, "who are we to question it?"

* * * * *

If you loved this baby story from
USA TODAY bestselling author
Michelle Celmer pick up

PLAYING BY THE BABY RULES
THE NANNY BOMBSHELL
PRINCESS IN THE MAKING

Available now from Harlequin Desire!
And don't miss the next
BILLIONAIRES AND BABIES story
THE BABY CONTRACT
from New York Times bestselling
author Barbara Dunlop
Available September 2015!

If you're on Twitter, tell us what you think of
Harlequin Desire! #harlequindesire

REQUEST YOUR FREE BOOKS!
2 FREE NOVELS PLUS 2 FREE GIFTS!

ⒽHARLEQUIN®

Desire

ALWAYS POWERFUL, PASSIONATE AND PROVOCATIVE

YES! Please send me 2 FREE Harlequin® Desire novels and my 2 FREE gifts (gifts are worth about $10). After receiving them, if I don't wish to receive any more books, I can return the shipping statement marked "cancel." If I don't cancel, I will receive 6 brand-new novels every month and be billed just $4.55 per book in the U.S. or $5.24 per book in Canada. That's a savings of at least 13% off the cover price! It's quite a bargain! Shipping and handling is just 50¢ per book in the U.S. and 75¢ per book in Canada.* I understand that accepting the 2 free books and gifts places me under no obligation to buy anything. I can always return a shipment and cancel at any time. Even if I never buy another book, the two free books and gifts are mine to keep forever.

225/326 HDN GH2P

Name _____ (PLEASE PRINT)

Address _____ Apt. #

City _____ State/Prov. _____ Zip/Postal Code

Signature (if under 18, a parent or guardian must sign)

Mail to the **Reader Service:**
IN U.S.A.: P.O. Box 1867, Buffalo, NY 14240-1867
IN CANADA: P.O. Box 609, Fort Erie, Ontario L2A 5X3

Want to try two free books from another line?
Call 1-800-873-8635 or visit www.ReaderService.com.

* Terms and prices subject to change without notice. Prices do not include applicable taxes. Sales tax applicable in N.Y. Canadian residents will be charged applicable taxes. Offer not valid in Quebec. This offer is limited to one order per household. Not valid for current subscribers to Harlequin Desire books. All orders subject to credit approval. Credit or debit balances in a customer's account(s) may be offset by any other outstanding balance owed by or to the customer. Please allow 4 to 6 weeks for delivery. Offer available while quantities last.

Your Privacy—The Reader Service is committed to protecting your privacy. Our Privacy Policy is available online at www.ReaderService.com or upon request from the Reader Service.

We make a portion of our mailing list available to reputable third parties that offer products we believe may interest you. If you prefer that we not exchange your name with third parties, or if you wish to clarify or modify your communication preferences, please visit us at www.ReaderService.com/consumerschoice or write to us at Reader Service Preference Service, P.O. Box 9062, Buffalo, NY 14240-9062. Include your complete name and address.

HDI5

Isabella was somehow even more beautiful than he'd
remembered. And probably more treacherous, Marc
reminded himself as he fought for control.

It had been six years since he'd seen her.

Six years since he'd held her, kissed her, made love
to her.

Six years since he'd kicked her out of his apartment
and his life.

And still, he wanted her.

It came as something of a shock, considering he'd
done his best not to think about her in the ensuing years.

All it had taken was a glimpse of her gorgeous red hair,
her warm brown eyes, from the small window embedded
in the classroom door to throw him right back into the
seething, tumultuous heat that had characterized so much
of their relationship. He hadn't cared about anything
but getting into that room to see if his mind was playing
tricks on him.

Six years ago he had kicked Isa Varin—now, apparently,
Isabella Moreno—out of his life in the cruelest manner
possible. He didn't regret making her leave—how could

HDEXP0815

he when she'd betrayed him so completely?—but in the time since, he had regretted how he'd done it. When he'd come to his senses and sent his driver to find her and deliver her things, including her purse and cell phone and some money, she had vanished into thin air. He'd looked for her, but he'd never found her.

Now he knew why. The very passionate, very beautiful, very bewitching Isa Varin had ceased to exist. In her place was this buttoned-down professor, her voice and face as cool and sharp as any diamond his mines had ever produced. Only the hair—that glorious red hair—was the same. Isabella Moreno wore it in a tight braid down her back instead of in the wild curls favored by his Isa, but he would know the color anywhere.

Black cherries at midnight.

Wet garnets shining in the filtered light of a full moon.

And when her eyes had met his over the heads of her students, he'd felt a punch in his gut—in his groin—that couldn't be denied. Only Isa had ever made his body react so powerfully.

One look into her eyes used to bring him to his knees. But those days were long gone. Her betrayal had destroyed any faith he might have had in her. He'd been weak once, had fallen for the innocence she could project with a look, a touch, a whisper.

He wouldn't make that mistake again.

Will Marc have Isa back in his bed, trust be damned?

Find out in CLAIMED, the first of the DIAMOND TYCOONS duet by New York Times bestselling author Tracy Wolff, available wherever Harlequin® Desire books and ebooks are sold.

www.Harlequin.com

THE WORLD IS BETTER WITH

Romance

Harlequin has everything from contemporary, passionate and heartwarming to suspenseful and inspirational stories.

Whatever your mood,
we have a romance just for you!

Connect with us to find your next great read, special offers and more.

f /HarlequinBooks

🐦 @HarlequinBooks

www.HarlequinBlog.com

www.Harlequin.com/Newsletters

❖ HARLEQUIN®

A *Romance* FOR EVERY MOOD™

www.Harlequin.com